Falling For You

A Thanksgiving Novella

Marissa James

This book is dedicated to all the readers who just want a fun short holiday
read.
Enjoy!

<h1 style="text-align:center;">Synopsis</h1>

Who says Thanksgiving isn't the perfect time to fall in love?

My Thanksgiving plans were simple: eat a frozen pizza, watch reruns of my favorite show, read, and knit. It didn't bother me that I would spend the holiday alone. But my roommate wouldn't hear of it and convinced me to go to her parent's house with her.

I never expected to run into her twin brother - Thatcher Wells - on Thanksgiving morning. It's been fifteen years since I last saw him, and apparently, I never got over the crush I had on him in college.

As a newly divorced woman, I thought I was destined to be alone. That is until Thatcher walks back into my life. It feels like the universe is giving me a second chance at love with someone who listens to me and puts me first. Something my ex didn't do.

I just hope it's not too good to be true.

Tropes: Roommate's Brother.
Intended for audiences 18+. Contains open door scenes.

Chapter 1

Avery

"I can't believe you're planning to eat a frozen pizza for Thanksgiving," Caroline says from across the table, a plate of half-eaten scrambled eggs and toast in front of her.

"It's not that big of a deal, Caro. My parents are going on a cruise. I've got some books I've been dying to read and a knitting project to keep me busy."

"You should come home with me," she says, taking a sip of her coffee.

"No, I couldn't do that." I shake my head before taking another bite of my scrambled eggs. "I appreciate it, but I'll be fine here."

"The holidays are for spending time with family or friends. Not being alone. Come home with me."

"I'll be fine, Caro, but thank you. I'm not really a fan of turkey so it's not like I'm sad to be missing out on that." I hold my breath, hoping she'll drop it. It really doesn't bother me to spend the holiday alone.

"Psssh. The more the merrier is what Ma always says. She won't mind." She waves her hand around. "We don't even eat turkey." She grins at me, and I swallow my groan. "I think we're having a roast this year instead. Please. Please. Do it for me." Caro puts her hands together and pretends to beg, attempting to give me sad puppy dog eyes. "My parents are less likely to ask about my dating life if you're there. They'll be on their best behavior."

"So the truth comes out." I know she's being nice and would probably have invited me anyway, but it seems she has an ulterior motive. "What's in it for me?" I ask, arching my eyebrows at her.

"I'll clean the kitchen for the rest of the year. I know you hate doing it."

I tip my head, studying my roommate. "You're that desperate for me to come with you?"

"Yes." She huffs out a breath. "Neither of my brothers will be there, which means I'll be the sole focus of my parents' attention. My mother loves trying to find one of her friends' sons to set me up with. It's a nightmare." She rolls her eyes. "When I was there in September for her birthday, one of her friends dropped by and *conveniently* her son was with her."

I bite back a laugh. "Have you tried telling them you're not interested?"

"Plenty of times. They don't listen. I've even tried to tell them I was seeing someone. They didn't buy it." She throws her hands up in mock outrage.

I shake my head, chuckling. I've known her for nearly a year and I've never seen her go out with the same guy more than twice. I swear dating is her hobby. I can easily count the number of dates I've been on this year—hint: it's a big fat zero—while she goes on at least one a week. Don't get me wrong, that's fine, it's just not for me.

My divorce was finalized over the summer, but it's only been in the past few weeks that I've thought about dating again. I finally feel like I'm ready to get back out there. As scary as it sounds, I think it will be my New Year's resolution. Seems fitting I mark the anniversary of when I moved here by starting to date again. Yep, I did what any other thirty-five-year-old would do after she gets divorced from her husband of five years. I packed my car up and moved to a new state. That sounds way more dramatic than it really was.

In all actuality my job offered me a promotion the week after I filed for divorce. It meant moving to North Carolina where the marketing firm I work for is headquartered since I would be moving from a remote role to an on-site client facing one. If I hadn't been getting divorced, I wouldn't have accepted it because Chad, my ex, would never have agreed to leave Tennessee and his family, nor would he have even considered working remotely, even though his job allowed it. But I was a free woman and it felt like a sign from the universe that I was making the right decision divorcing Chad, so I took the job.

What I didn't take into account was that even though the promotion came with a nice pay raise, Idlewild is expensive, and living alone in a nice area is impossible. Enter Jane, my friend and coworker who happened to know Caroline, and knew she was looking for a roommate. She introduced us. The rest is history. Caro and I may only have met eleven months ago, but I swear it's like we've known each other forever.

"Earth to Avery." Caro waves her hands around, and I blink a few times trying to figure out what I missed. She shakes her head at me. "They're up in Maple Ridge Valley, which is a few hours drive. My plan is to drive there Wednesday evening and come home on Friday morning."

"Okay fine," I concede. "I'll go with you as long as you're sure your parents won't mind."

"Yes!" She fist pumps the air, grabbing her phone off the table. "They won't. I promise. But I'll text them now if it'll make you feel better."

"It would. Let me know what they say. I need to get ready for work." I take my dirty dishes to the sink, rinse them off, and then put them in the almost full dishwasher, making a mental note to turn it on after dinner tonight.

Twenty minutes later I'm grabbing my laptop bag and purse from their spots in the corner of my bedroom before making my way into the kitchen to fill up my water bottle and pour another cup of coffee into my travel mug.

"Bye," I yell to Caro as I walk toward the front door.

"See ya." She waves to me from her spot on the couch, her laptop perched on her lap.

She owns her own social media management company and works from the comfort of the apartment in her pajamas every day. Some days I wish I could still do that, like I did before my promotion, but it is nice to interact with coworkers in person. I still get to work from home occasionally. I would have done that this week, but I agreed to have lunch with Jane today, and my team is having a potluck tomorrow.

As I'm navigating my sedan into a parking space in front of the office, my phone pings. After putting the car in park, I grab it and read a message from my mom.

Mom:

> I hope you have a great day. Have you decided what you're doing for Thanksgiving?

Me:

> Yep. Caroline invited me to go home with her. Her family lives a few hours away.

Good. Make sure you bring something. Do you want me to send you my pumpkin pie recipe? It's easy and always a crowd pleaser. Or my stuffing recipe. That's a good option.

I chuckle. Leave it to my mom and her southern hospitality.

I was planning to bring a couple of bottles of wine with me. But send me the pie recipe please.

With a smile, I tuck my phone into my purse, gather up my things, and get out of the car. Now that I have plans for the holiday, I'm actually excited. Two and a half days of work to get through first, but then it'll be a relaxing few days.

I hope.

I'm sure it'll be great spending the holiday with Caro's family.

Chapter 2

Thatcher

"I don't know, Mom," I mutter into the phone, running a hand down my face.

"Please, Thatch. Do it for me. Hudson called this morning to say he's coming home. I want to have all my babies in one place for the holiday. It's been years."

I groan. I should have hit Ignore when I saw my mom was calling. I don't have time for this. I'm in the middle of working on an update to a client's mobile application. It should have been an easy update, but of course it's become more complicated. Which means it's taking more time than I anticipated.

I love my parents, I really do.

And my siblings.

I just don't have time to take a day–or two–off right now for Thanksgiving. I'd planned to work through the holiday so I could get this project finished. I'm also in the middle of developing a game for a second client that needs to go to beta testers in a few weeks, and I'm not where I need to be with that.

"Please, Thatch," she repeats. "I'm planning to make a roast. And your favorite mashed potatoes and mac and cheese."

I sigh. I haven't seen my parents since Christmas. I haven't seen my younger brother in over a year because he's been touring with his band. I do some mental math, trying to figure out how much work I need to get done between now and Thursday so that after the holiday, I'm not even more behind.

I blow out a breath. "Okay, but it'll have to be a quick visit."

"I'll take whatever I can get. I can't wait to have all my babies in one place." I can hear the happiness in my mom's voice, and I know that I made the right decision even if it means a lot of late nights and early mornings for the foreseeable future.

"I've got to go get work done. I'll see you Thursday."

"Bye, honey. See you soon."

"Bye Mom."

I hang up the phone and sink into the couch, leaning my head against the wall and trying not to panic about everything I need to get done in the next few days. Shadow decides that now is a good time to jump up and curl up in my lap.

Which he never does.

I swear he always knows when something is up with me. I pet him and he purrs. I adopted him a few years ago from the local animal shelter. When I walked in and saw him, I knew he was the cat for me. Don't ask me how. I just did. He apparently agreed because he let me pick him up with almost no fuss. Something the volunteers said he wouldn't let anyone else do. We've been best friends ever since. Even though he ignores me most of the time unless I'm offering him catnip or a treat or when he somehow knows that I'm stressing out.

I sit for a few more minutes with Shadow in my lap, breathing deeply before getting to my feet and heading into my office to work.

On Wednesday morning an alert pings on my phone telling me that the weather for tomorrow is forecast to be bad. They're predicting strong thunderstorms and possible hail here in Greenwood with the potential for flooding. I had planned to get up early and make the four-hour drive to my parents' on Thanksgiving morning, stay overnight, and leave early Friday. But the forecast is making me rethink my plans, especially because the drive through the mountains to Maple Ridge Valley is winding and very narrow in places. Parts of the road flood. I don't want to make the drive in bad weather *and* holiday traffic. Guess I'm driving down tonight.

I send my mom a quick text to let her know my change in plans before burying myself in work for most of the day. Around five, I finally power off my laptop, make myself a quick sandwich for dinner, throw some clothes and toiletries into an overnight bag, check Shadow's automatic food and water bowls as well as his litter, and head out the door.

It's after ten when I pull into the driveway and park behind Caro's hatchback. Taking a deep breath, I turn my car off, grab my bags from the backseat, and make my way up the front walkway. All the while saying a silent prayer that everyone didn't decide to stay up late to see me, because I'm tired and want to go to bed.

I'm greeted by a quiet house when I let myself in with my key, and I breathe a sigh of relief. I make my way into the kitchen, needing a drink and maybe a snack before I go to bed. Between getting up early for work all week and driving tonight, I'm exhausted. On the counter is a note. I set my bags down and read it.

Thatch

Made up the bed in your old room. Hope the drive was okay. See you in the morning.

Love,

Mom

"Hey." My sister's voice comes from behind me.

"Hey Caro," I say, turning to her.

"Who are you?" she asks playfully as she hugs me. "Are you my twin? Because I haven't seen him in ages, even though we live an hour away from each other."

"Very funny," I grumble, letting her go. She steps back and leans against the counter.

"You look good," I say, taking my sister in. Her dyed auburn hair is thrown into a messy bun on the top of her head. For whatever reason, she never did like her natural, brown hair that matches mine. In high school and college, she dyed it all kinds of different colors until she settled on the auburn. She's wearing black leggings with a rip in one knee and an oversized shirt.

"It's all the yoga and meditation I've been doing."

"Since when do you do yoga?"

She shrugs before stepping around me to the cabinet and grabbing a glass. "If you were around more, you'd know I picked it up a few months ago. Anyway, I came down to get a glass of water. Want one?"

"Sure." I take the glass from her.

"Oh, one of my friends came with me. So don't be walking around the house in only your boxers in the morning. She'll be mortified." Caro fills another glass with water and takes a drink before meeting my gaze. Her brown eyes, the same color as Mom's, are sparkling with mischief. I raise my eyebrows at her, my twin spidey senses tingling.

"Good to know. Not that I'd ever do that here."

"You never know," Caro says before grabbing another glass and filling it up. For her friend, I assume. "Hudson isn't here yet. His flight was delayed. Last I checked, he's supposed to get in around midnight."

I nod while she wanders over to the cabinet and grabs a bag of pretzels. "We're watching a movie in my room if you want to join us."

"Thanks, but I think I'm going to shower and head to bed. I've been up since four."

"Suit yourself. Night, little brother. It's good to see you."

"Night."

I finish my water and put the glass in the dishwasher, grab my bags, make sure the front door is locked, and head upstairs, leaving the light on for Hudson.

As I fall asleep, it occurs to me that I didn't ask Caro about her friend. I don't even know the woman's name. I make a mental note to be a better brother tomorrow and ask about her life. To make an effort to be more involved with her. Maybe she and I can make plans to meet up at a coffee shop and work together since we both work from home. Or a coworking space we could rent for the day.

Chapter 3

Avery

Rubbing my eyes, I sit up in bed, trying not to disturb Caro who's still sleeping next to me. I was supposed to stay in Caro's twin brother's room, but it turned out he was coming home last night instead of this morning because of the nasty storms, and I didn't want to take his bed. Caro's youngest brother was also going to be home, so his room was spoken for. So much for Caro telling me none of her siblings were going to be here.

It's fine. It's okay. Doesn't really change anything.

Beth, Caro's mom, insisted that one of her sons could sleep on the pull-out couch in the den, but I felt bad putting someone out. Caro offered to share her queen bed with me. It's not the first time we've shared a bed—we took a weekend trip a few months ago to Asheville, and the hotel screwed up, and we ended up having to share then.

"It's really storming," Caro mumbles as she rolls onto her back.

"Yeah, it is. I'm glad we don't have to drive in it," I answer just as thunder booms, shaking the whole house.

She sits up and rolls her shoulders, stretching her upper body. "Do you need the bathroom before I go in there to get ready?"

"No, I'm good." I grab my phone from the nightstand as she hops out of bed and makes her way into the en suite.

She said this room used to be her parents' bedroom until they decided to add another primary bedroom downstairs when it was clear that her brothers needed their own space. I wonder what it was like growing up with not just siblings but a twin too. As an only child, I've always been envious of those with siblings. Built-in friends. Someone to always have your back. At least, when I was a child that's what I imagined it would be like.

I absentmindedly scroll through social media while I wait for my turn in the bathroom. Everyone I know is either married, engaged, or having kids, and while I know everyone has their own path in life, it still makes me sad.

Sad that my marriage to Chad didn't last. I thought he was my one, the guy I'd spend the rest of my life with. And he wasn't. I'm glad I found that out now instead of in ten or twenty years but still, we'd been married for five years and dated for three before that. A lot of my adult life was spent with someone who is now no longer part of it.

"Whatcha thinking about?"

I startle at the sound of Caroline's voice. "Nothing. Just life. Getting older."

"Holidays do put it in perspective, remind you that you're single." She gestures toward my phone. "But we're not thinking about that today. Today is the day for eating too much food and having a good time. Bathroom's all yours."

"What should I wear?" I ask as I make my way from the bed to my overnight bag, sitting on a chair in the corner of the room.

"I'm gonna change into a pair of leggings and a shirt. Nothing fancy. We'll probably lounge around all day, watch the Macy's Day Parade. If it was nice out, we could walk over to the park but not in this storm."

I grab a pair of black joggers, my favorite faded long-sleeve purple shirt, and my toiletry bag and head into the bathroom.

"Ready for coffee?" Caro asks a few minutes later when I walk back into the bedroom.

"Yeah," I say, following her out of the bedroom and downstairs.

"Good morning," Beth says from her seat at the table as we step into the kitchen. "There's biscuits and gravy on the counter. And a fresh pot of coffee. I can whip up some eggs too."

"Morning," Caro singsongs, beelining for the coffee pot. She grabs two mugs from the cabinet and pours coffee into each one.

"Good morning. Thanks." I take the mug that Caro hands me.

"Hey, Ma. Sis." A male voice comes from behind me.

"Hudson," Beth exclaims, getting to her feet.

I turn toward the voice, and my mouth falls open. Caro's little brother is Blaze, the lead singer of Burning Bridges. No way. I blink a few times, wondering if I'm imagining things.

"Hud," Caro says, her eyes lighting up, as she eagerly walks over to where her brother and mother are hugging.

"Caroline," he says his voice cracking, giving her a once over before putting his arms out to her.

The more I stare at them all together, the more I can see the family resemblance. He's got the same brown eyes as Caro and her mother do and the same nose. I can't believe I didn't see it before. But why would I even consider that Caro could be related to a rock star?

"Who do we have here?" he asks, flashing me a megawatt smile, the one that probably melts thousands of panties.

He's cute with his long brown hair and dimples, but he's not my type.

"That's Avery, my roommate," Caro says.

"H–Hi," I stutter out, setting my mug down.

Caro shakes her head, chuckling. "You're a fan aren't you."

I blush. "I've listened to their music a time or two."

Hudson huffs out a laugh. I finally gather myself and put out a hand to him. "Nice to meet you."

He gives a small shake of his head before tugging me into a hug.

I bite my lip to hold in the giggle that wants to escape.

I will not fangirl.

I will not fangirl. I'm a thirty-five-year-old woman, damn it.

I will not fangirl over him.

I'm hugging Blaze from Burning Bridges.

"Hudson," Caro says sternly.

I awkwardly pat him on the back. "Nice to meet you, Hudson." I make a mental note to yell at Caro later for not warning me about her brother being a rock star.

"You too, Avery," he says, letting me go and taking a step back. "What's for breakfast? I'm starving." He pats his stomach as he glances around the kitchen.

Beth jumps into action. When we each have a plate full of eggs, bacon, biscuits, and gravy, we take seats around the kitchen table.

"Where's Dad?" Hudson asks between bites.

Beth sighs. "He's out in the garage tinkering with the generator. I told him we weren't going to need it. But it's storming, and you know how your father gets."

Hudson nods, continuing to eat. The rest of the meal passes in silence, and pretty soon the table is cleared, and Caro and I are the only ones still in the kitchen.

"I'm going to run upstairs and put some socks on," I tell Caro as she pours herself another cup of coffee. I didn't think about how cold the tile floor would be when I got dressed this morning, and my feet have been freezing all through breakfast.

"I'm going to take this"—she holds up her full coffee mug—"and go turn the parade on in the living room."

"Okay. I'll be right back."

As I'm making my way down the hallway toward Caro's room, my phone dings, and I unlock it to read my mom's text and run straight into a wall.

"Owww." I groan, rubbing my forehead.

"You okay?" the wall, which isn't a wall, asks, and I jump back in shock, stumbling over my own feet. "Careful," the guy, who must be Caro's twin, says, reaching out to steady me.

My mouth opens and closes a few times as I stare up into the familiar green eyes partially hidden by a pair of glasses that I'd know anywhere.

"Thanks," I whisper, finally finding my voice.

A slow smile graces his face, a dimple peeking out, as his eyes rake over me, probably checking for injury.

I don't wait for him to say something else. Instead, I turn on my heel and all but run into Caroline's room, slamming the door behind me.

How did I not know Caroline's twin was none other than the guy I had a crush on in college—Thatcher Wells?

The guy I was supposed to go on a date with during senior year the week that Hurricane Linda swept through south Florida and closed campus for three weeks. I'd had a crush on him for a while, and I was so excited when he finally asked me out, except a hurricane had to come though.

When campus reopened, classes were hectic, trying to make up for the lost time so the semester didn't have to be extended. It felt like a sign from the universe that we weren't meant to be, so I didn't pursue it. And he didn't pursue me, so I figured he agreed.

It might be almost fifteen years since the last time I saw him, but apparently the man is like Paul Rudd—he doesn't age. He looks almost the same as he did in our last class together, spring semester of senior year. He's even wearing the same glasses. Well, I'm sure not the *same* glasses, just similar frames. But still.

Caro and I have known each other for a year, and I've never seen pictures of her brothers as adults. For whatever reason the only photo of her family hanging in the living room is a picture of her and her siblings at Disney World when they were little. Oddly enough *all* the photos in her room are either her and her siblings when they were younger or her with just her parents.

Today has most definitely been an interesting day, and it's not even noon.

Chapter 4

Thatcher

I stare at the closed door of my sister's room for far too long. What the hell is Avery Butler doing here? The literal woman of my dreams. The one I've compared every woman I've ever dated to. Which is crazy because we never even went out on a date. But she's here now.

Why?

Shaking myself out of my Avery-induced haze, I head toward the stairs and take them two at a time.

She's got to be Caro's friend. Hudson's never brought a woman home, so I doubt he'd start now. Plus she went into Caro's old room. So clearly not with Hudson. Caroline is friends with Avery? What a small world.

"Caro," I call as I stride into the living room.

"Hey, little brother," she greets me from her seat on the couch.

I roll my eyes at her, she's barely five minutes older than I am. Hardly grounds for being the little brother. I glance around the room, grateful that the rest of the family is somewhere else.

"Ma is in her bedroom. Dad's out in the garage. I don't know where Hudson went," she says as if reading my mind, which she probably did because of the whole twin thing.

"Actually, it's you I was looking for," I say, taking a seat next to her. "I ran into your *friend* upstairs."

"Oh, Avery. My roommate. You didn't scare her away, did you?" Caro asks, sitting up straight and pinning me with a look.

"No." I swallow. "I didn't. Why would you think I would? Wait." I hold up a hand, frowning. "Since when do you have a roommate? You told me she was your friend."

"She's both. For almost a year now," she says with a shrug. "Rent went up, I didn't want to move, so I got a roommate. You'd know that if you were around more."

I shake my head. "What's she doing here?"

"She didn't have anywhere else to go so I invited her. Ma was fine with it."

I nod. That makes sense. Still weird that Avery is here. In my parents' house. If I had to guess, by the way she reacted, she recognized me. But why did she run away? I lean back against the couch.

I feel Caro watching me and turn to meet her stare. "What?"

"You're being weird." She waves a hand around, one eyebrow raised. "Why are you asking about my roommate?"

I heave out a breath. Do I tell her? Do I not tell her? I settle on half the story. "Avery and I went to college together. It was a surprise to see her after all these years."

"Good or bad surprise?" Caro frowns, picking up her coffee mug from the side table.

"Good."

"So?" She tilts her head, studying me over her steaming mug.

"So nothing. I was surprised. Caught off guard."

Caro continues studying me in silence, and I get the distinct impression that she can see right through me. The one time in my life that I wish we weren't twins. I stand before she can say anything. Call me out for not telling her the entire story.

"I'm going to get some breakfast." I need to get out of here before she weasels everything out of me. I give her what I hope is an intimidating look over my shoulder. "Can you please not say anything to Avery? About me recognizing her from college."

Caro dips her chin in agreement. Wordlessly I walk into the kitchen and fix myself a plate of leftover biscuits, gravy, and the last few pieces of bacon.

All the regret that I never tried harder to reschedule our date comes back to the surface as I eat.

We had English Lit together that semester and were even in the same study group. The campus wasn't that big; we ran into each other all the time. When campus reopened, I was swamped with assignments, and so was she. We tried to reschedule our date, but things kept coming up. I didn't push it because I figured she was too nice to tell me she didn't want to date me after all. I regretted it for the rest of the year, but I never had time to dwell on it. Senior year as a computer science major meant a lot of late nights and weekends in the computer lab completing coding projects.

I don't even know if she remembers me.

Why would she? I'm just a guy she almost dated.

Fifteen years ago.

"You okay?" Hudson asks, breaking into my thoughts.

"Yeah, why?" I answer before taking a bite of my biscuits and gravy that have now gone cold.

"I've been standing here saying your name, and you didn't answer." He watches me from his spot by the kitchen sink, a glass of orange juice in his hand.

"Sorry. Guess I spaced out. I'm tired." The lie slips off my tongue easily.

"How are things? How's the business?"

"The business is good. Busy, but I enjoy it."

"That's great, brother. Are you still a one-man show?"

"How's the band?" I ask, changing the subject. Of course I'm still a one-man show. I don't trust anyone else. Not after what happened last time I trusted someone enough to be in business with them.

Hudson launches into a story about Knox, the band's drummer, and some prank he pulled on Nash, one of their other bandmates. I try to pay attention, muttering my surprise in all the right places as I eat the rest of my breakfast.

"Alright boys," Mom says, coming into the kitchen and interrupting our conversation. "I'm going to start prepping for dinner."

"Need help?" Hudson asks.

"Maybe later. I'll let you know. Hi, Thatch, baby." She greets me with a kiss on the cheek and a pat on my shoulder then takes my empty plate to the sink.

"I could have done that," I protest.

"I know, but I got it." She gives us both a pointed look, and we take the hint that she wants us out of the kitchen.

We always offer to help, but she likes to do things a certain way and says she enjoys doing all the cooking. We pitch in when she lets us—making a salad or helping with the side dishes—but we've stopped arguing with her about letting us help more.

"It's good to have you home," I tell my brother as we make our way into the living room.

The ladies are sitting on the couch, their heads close together as they chat. The Macy's Day Parade is on the television, the sound muted. I relax into the loveseat next to Hudson, trying and failing to stop myself from staring at the beauty sitting with my sister.

I didn't get much of a chance to check out Avery when I ran into her upstairs, so I do it now. I may not be able to get a full view of her, but from what I can see, she's as gorgeous as I remember. Maybe even more so.

Hudson clears his throat, and Caro and Avery look up.

"Oh, you're here. Good." Caro says, clapping her hands. "This is my roommate, Avery." She points at Avery. "You finally get to meet my twin, Thatcher. We call him Thatch. You already met Hudson."

"Nice to meet you," Avery says, putting her hand out to me.

I lean forward and take it. Her hand is warm and soft in mine. I want to tug her into my lap. Or pull her out of the room and ask if she knows who I am. If she remembers me. But I don't do any of that. Because that would be creepy. Instead, I give her another smile before letting go of her hand.

"What's it like to be in a band?" she asks, turning to face Hudson.

I sigh, bracing myself for the stories I've heard a million times over.

"A lot of work," he says, but before he can say anything else, his phone rings. He frowns at it before getting to his feet. "Sorry. I have to get this. It's my manager. Must be an emergency if he's calling on Thanksgiving." With that, he walks out of the room.

I turn my attention to Avery, but before I can speak, Caro says, "Oh, how's my nephew? Do you have any new photos of him?"

Chapter 5

Avery

My heart drops at the mention of a nephew. Of course Thatcher has kids. Does that mean he's married? He's not wearing a wedding band. Maybe they're not together. When Caro introduced us, I wanted to blurt out that we went to college together. But I couldn't. Besides, what does it matter now? He's got a kid. Not that I'm against dating a single father. Why am I even thinking about dating him? For all I know, he's in a relationship. I give myself a mental shake and focus on the conversation.

"Shadow is doing good," Thatcher says, leaning forward to show Caro something on his phone before turning the screen so I can see it too.

My heart skips a beat at the photo of a black cat sitting on a desk, staring straight into the camera as if he knows his photo is being taken and is posing. *He's a cat dad? Why does that make him even sexier?*

"You should have brought him," Caro says.

"Nah. He's fine. He's got an automatic food and water bowl. Plus one of those self-cleaning kitty litters. Mr. Jacobs from next door promised to check on him tonight."

Caro laughs. "I'm surprised you don't have one of those pet camera things."

"Oh, I do." He taps something on his phone before turning to show us his screen again. The video is grainy, but you can make out a cat house thing with a cat sleeping on top of it.

"Love it," Caro says. "If I'd known you were coming, I would have picked up some treats for my nephew."

"That cat is spoiled. He doesn't need more treats."

The conversation shifts, and I relax on the couch as the two siblings catch up, taking the time to check Thatcher out more than the glimpse I got upstairs.

His brown hair isn't styled, unlike Chad's, which was always perfect—he spent more time on his hair than I did. No, Thatcher's hair looks like he ran his hand through it when he woke up, and that was it. He's wearing black frame glasses not unlike the ones he wore when we were in college.

His taste in clothing has changed though. He's swapped his superhero shirts for a green Henley. Although perhaps he still has those shirts and just dressed up because it's the holiday. I didn't mind his superhero shirts back then, and I most certainly wouldn't mind them now. And his jeans fit him perfectly. At least, from my position they do. Not that I was checking him out, out of the corner of my eye when he walked in.

I tilt my head, studying him some more, my gaze glued to his biceps, which flex when he rests his arm along the back of the couch. A throat clearing has me blinking, and I look up into the twinkling green eyes of Thatcher, who's watching me, his lips twitching as he tries to hold back a smile or laugh. He winks at me before turning to his sister, who's asking him something about his business.

Shaking myself out of my Thatcher-induced stupor, I get to my feet. "You alright?" Caro asks, turning to me.

"Fine. I should probably go call my parents."

She stares at me for a beat, and I wonder if she caught on to me checking out her brother, but she simply nods and goes back to her conversation. I hurry out of the room to make my phone call. And maybe hide in the bedroom for a little while.

"And that's how we ended up signing with Emporium Records," Hudson says, finishing his story, which I'm sure his family has heard a million times based on how often Caro sighed during it. Beth kept shooting her looks from across the table.

"That's cool," I answer before taking another bite of Beth's delicious roast.

I didn't realize asking Hudson about his band would result in a whole ten-minute spiel from him.

"How long are you in town for?" Chris, Caro's father, asks Hudson before he can launch into another anecdote, and for that, I'm grateful.

"A few days. We have some shows on the West Coast before we wrap up the week before Christmas."

"Does that mean you'll be home for Christmas?" Beth perks up.

"Yep."

She claps her hands together and lets out a little squeal. Hudson grins at his mom before spooning another bite of mashed potatoes into his mouth.

As dinner is wrapping up, Beth turns to Caro and says, "My friend Maria's son is in town. I thought I might invite them over for brunch tomorrow, since you said you wanted to be on the road by noon, so you can meet him."

My eyes about pop out of my head. I thought Caro was kidding when she said her mom was always trying to play matchmaker.

"No, that's okay, Ma. But thanks." Caro shakes her head, stabbing at the last piece of broccoli on her plate with a little more force than necessary.

"Oh, it's no big deal, honey."

"Ma, I said no. I'm quite capable of getting my own dates. I have one tomorrow night."

"Are you still using those apps to meet guys? I think you should try the old-fashioned way. It worked for your father and I." Beth turns to gaze lovingly at Chris, who looks at her just as fondly.

I peek over at Thatcher and Hudson who are both adamantly paying attention. Caro stays silent, staring at her plate. You could cut the tension with a knife, and I'm having secondhand embarrassment that I'm witnessing this.

"So, Avery, what is it you do for a living?" Hudson asks, finally breaking the silence.

I tuck a stray piece of hair behind my ear before answering. "Nothing as exciting as being a rock star. I work in marketing. I help our clients with new product launches or rebranding. Things like that." I wave my hand around.

"You've lived in North Carolina for a year now?" Beth asks.

"Yep, almost a year. When my divorce was finalized, I needed a new start, plus Appleton, where I moved from, is tiny and it's my ex's hometown. I knew I'd run into him or his family, so I took a promotion that meant moving here." I stare at my empty plate, not wanting to see what I'm sure are the looks of pity on everyone's faces.

"And met me, the best roommate ever," Caro adds, reaching over to squeeze my hand as if she can sense my unease at talking about my ex.

Everyone laughs, and I give her a weak grin, grateful to her for defusing the tension caused by the very serious bomb I dropped on her family. Why I chose to tell them I'm divorced is beyond me.

You know why, so Thatcher will know you're single.

I push that thought away.

I barely know the guy. Heck, I barely knew the guy when we were in college. Who knows what he's like now. What he's into. If he's even interested in me.

But that's what dating is for.

But maybe he's dating someone.

As if she can tell I'm rabbitholing, Caro nudges me and gestures for my empty plate. I hand it to her, and she stacks it on top of hers and stands to head into the kitchen. Everyone gets to their feet, and we make quick work of cleaning off the table while Hudson and Thatcher start washing the dishes.

Twenty minutes later, everyone is gathered in the living room. Caro told me that it's Thanksgiving tradition to watch *National Lampoon's Christmas Vacation* after dinner. I've seen the movie a few times, but I still get sucked into it like it's my first time watching it.

Before long, I hear snoring coming from the recliner in the corner where Chris is lounging. I glance at Caro and Beth to my right, and they both appear to be asleep. The guys on the loveseat don't look long for this world either. Hudson is leaning against the couch cushions, a blanket pulled up to his chin. There's no way he can see the television from that angle. Thatcher's glasses are on the coffee table, so I'd guess he's asleep or almost asleep too.

I watch for a little while longer before getting up and turning off the movie. I make my way upstairs, quietly so as to not wake anyone, grab my knitting, and head into the kitchen. I fill a glass with water from the sink before moving over to the table and pulling my current project out of my bag.

With a quick glance at the pattern and my scribbled notes to see what row I'm up to and how many knit and purl stitches I need for each block, I pull my knitting into my lap and start counting stitches being careful to keep the tension on the yarn just right so I don't end up with holes between stitches.

"What are you working on?"

I gasp and jump, banging my knee on the table.

"Shit," Thatcher says, hurrying over to me. "I'm sorry, I didn't mean to scare you. I thought you heard me come in."

I shake my head, blinking back the tears that are threatening to fall due to the pain in my knee.

"Did you get hurt? Do you need ice?" Thatcher gestures toward the freezer.

"I'll probably have a bruise, but I'm okay," I say, rubbing the spot I hit.

He nods, seemingly satisfied with my answer, then walks over to the fridge and peers inside. "Want a beer?" he asks, pulling out a bottle and turning to me. "Or there's wine."

"Beer's good."

He grabs another bottle before opening both of them and handing me one as he takes a seat at the table.

"What are you working on?"

I hold it up so he can see. "A blanket for my mom. For Christmas. Hopefully. If not, for her birthday in March." I'm rambling but I can't help it.

He takes a sip of his beer, and I do the same, watching him.

"We knew each other in college," he blurts out before slapping a hand over his mouth.

Chapter 6

Thatcher

Shit. Shit. Shit. I can't believe I said that. I had a whole plan—I was going to ask her about herself and then tell her she looked familiar. Guess that went out the window. I sip my beer, waiting to see what she says.

"I know, Thatch. I remember you. The date we never went on because of that fucking hurricane. I wanted to say something earlier but didn't know how."

I stare at her, unblinking. She knew. She remembers me. Me? The shy, quiet computer science major who somehow got up the courage to ask the gorgeous business major out, only to have the date ruined by Mother Nature.

"Well." I run a hand through my hair. "That's great!"

That's great? Really?

She takes a sip of her beer before saying, "Don't worry, I was as shocked as you when I ran into you. Why do you think I fled?"

I huff out a laugh, remembering the scene from this morning. Gosh, was it really this morning? It feels like it was weeks ago.

"Why don't we take these"—I hold up my beer bottle—"and go sit in the sunroom. It's more comfortable than here." I gesture to the kitchen chairs we're sitting on. "We can catch up."

"I'd like that." She puts her knitting into the bag that was sitting on the table and stands up.

I lead her through the house and into the sunroom. Pushing the door open, I flip on the fairy lights that Mom put up along the ceiling, which give off a soft glow. Enough light to see by but not blinding like the overhead light.

We take a seat on the couch, the only furniture in the room except the coffee table in front of it. The rest of the sunroom is taken over by Mom's plants that she's already brought in for the winter. The rain still pounding against the glass makes the room feel even more cozy.

How did I get so lucky to get a second chance with my dream girl? There's no way in hell I'm leaving tomorrow without her phone number. There won't be a repeat of the regrets of college and not having a way to get in contact with her.

"What have you been up to? How's life been since graduation?" Avery asks.

I proceed to tell her about Shadow, my company, and some of the projects I've worked on. I leave out that I'm a workaholic who barely has a social life, nor do I tell her about my first failed company. She doesn't need to know about that.

"What about you?" I ask. Although the question I really want to ask is *do you have a boyfriend?*

She shifts closer to me, her thigh brushing against mine, before telling me what she's been up to.

"Since I moved here, I don't do a whole lot. I should get out more, but I'm such a homebody. I don't really know many people here. It's hard to make friends as an adult." She pauses and I nod. "I have a few work friends that I go out with, but your sister is my closest friend. I usually just stay at home, knit, and hang out with your sister. I do watch a lot of hockey during the season. That takes up a lot of my time."

"Who do you root for?" I'm not a hockey fan by any means, but I saw the way her face lit up when she mentioned it.

She swirls her drink before taking a sip. "The Orlando Storm," she says once she's swallowed her beer.

"Cool." I take a sip from my own bottle, hoping she'll say more. I'm quickly finding I could listen to her talk all day. Something about her sweet voice is calming.

"Yeah, I know the Charlotte Wings are the local team, but I love the Storm. Growing up in Central Florida they were the local team, so of course, I became a fan. My dad and I went to a lot of games over the years." She waves her hand around, her fingers brushing against my arm, which breaks out in goosebumps. Fuck, I'm in trouble. "I haven't been to a game in years. I think they're in town soon. I should see if I can get tickets."

I hum in response. What am I supposed to say?

"What about you, Thatcher? Do you watch sports?" she asks, laying a hand on my arm. And I can't focus. The way my name rolls off her tongue. The way she's touching me. I give myself a mental shake.

"Not a big sports fan." I down the rest of my beer before putting the empty bottle on the coffee table. "Can I ask what happened between you and your ex to end the marriage?"

She stares at me silently for a few seconds, and I fear I've overstepped.

"I shouldn't have asked. If you don't want to talk about it . . ." I quickly add, hoping I didn't ruin the moment.

"No, it's okay." She shakes her head. "We never lived together before we got married, and I think that was our first mistake. It's one thing to date someone and spend weekends with them, but it's an entirely different thing when you live together and you see them all the time. You know what I mean?" She tilts her head, and I nod. I've never been in a long-term relationship, so I don't really know what she means, but I can imagine. "When we did, I think we realized there were sides to each other we didn't get along with. We tried to make it work. For five years. And by we, I mean me. Because he always expected me to compromise when there were things we disagreed on. Never him. His way was always the right way. Toward the end, he got a big promotion and was never home. That's when I realized I'd never be his priority."

"Wow. I'm sorry." I put my hand on her arm.

She puts her hand over mine, squeezing it. "Thanks."

Before I can figure out how to change the subject, bring us back to the levity that we had before, Caro flings the door open.

"There you are." She steps into the sunroom. "Ma wants to have dessert. She sent me to find you both."

"You found us," Avery says, standing and grabbing her empty beer bottle from the table. "Dessert sounds great."

"Yeah," I agree, even though all I want to do is tell my sister to get lost so I can talk to Avery alone for longer.

I follow them to the kitchen where everyone is gathered around the table, which is covered in an array of dishes from pumpkin pie to cheesecake, and even brownies.

"Come sit," Mom says when we walk into the room.

Caro, Avery, and I cram along one side of the table with Mom, Dad, and Hudson on the other side. Dessert is passed around.

Because I'm left-handed and ended up sitting in the middle, Avery and I are constantly bumping elbows, exchanging grins when we do as we both eat a slice of pumpkin pie. Normally, it would annoy me, but I find myself purposely grazing her arm.

"Who's up for a game of Monopoly?" Caro asks after we've finished.

I groan silently. She loves Monopoly, and it isn't my idea of a good time, but I always get roped into playing.

"I'm in," Avery says.

"Me too," I find myself saying. If she's playing, I am too. Gives me an excuse to spend more time with her.

Mom agrees to join us, so once dessert is cleared away, the game is set up. Dad escapes into the living room, probably to watch a football game, with Hudson trailing behind him. He ignored our sister's pleas to play. I'm not sure how he's immune to her. Maybe he's used to having women beg him for things so he's gotten good at saying no.

We set up the board, and everyone picks their pieces. As usual, Caro is the banker, and she doles out everyone's money. Avery goes first.

It turns out to be fun since Avery is as competitive as Caro, and the two bicker about the rules quite a few times. I have to bite my lip from laughing at how serious they're taking it. Avery's cute when she's fired up, and I spend quite a bit of my time watching her out of the corner of my eye. We're once again sitting next to each other, and her leg keeps bumping into mine. I swear I feel her watching me a few times, but when I look over at her, she's studying the board.

Mom yawns and glances up at the clock on the stove after we've been playing for a while. "Gosh, it's been two hours already. I think I'm going to head to bed, kids. I'm bankrupt anyway, and all my property is mortgaged. There's no way I can make it around again."

I chuckle, looking at the board, which is mostly covered with houses and hotels courtesy of my sister. I don't know how she does it, but she always wins or comes as close to winning as you can. I think Mom purposely doesn't try hard, but I've never been able to prove it, and she's never admitted it. I put a decent amount of effort into buying properties but always come up short.

Mom gives us all hugs, even Avery, before walking out of the kitchen. "Don't stay up too late."

"I'm out too," I say, pushing my property cards to the middle of the table.

"But you've still got money." Caro points at the small stack of bills in front of me.

"I forfeit. One of you can have it." I wave a hand at my sister and her friend.

Avery giggles. "I think I'm done too."

"Fine. You all are no fun."

We clean up the game, and Caro goes to put it away in the hallway closet.

"Want another beer?" I ask Avery, walking over to the fridge.

"Sure." She comes over and takes a bottle from me. "What are the chances that we run into each other again after all these years?"

I take a sip of my beer and lean against the counter across from her. "Must be the universe telling us we should have stayed in touch."

She mirrors me, taking a sip of her drink before setting it down. She swallows, and I can't help staring as her tongue darts out and swipes at the beer on her lips. I finally force myself to meet her gaze to find her eyes wide as she watches me. I take the two steps across the kitchen so I'm standing right in front of her. I don't know if it's the alcohol that's making me brave or if it's her, but I'm not questioning it.

"I have a confession," I whisper.

"What is it?" she asks, standing up straight so we're practically nose to nose.

"I regret that we never went out on that date. I tried to find you at graduation. I called you a few months later, but your number was disconnected."

"I didn't go to graduation and my phone got stolen a few weeks after so I had to get a new number."

I reach out and tuck a piece of hair that's fallen out of her braid behind her ear. My hand lingers on her chin, my finger running down her cheek. "I cursed myself for not trying harder to reschedule our date for a really long time. I tried to find you on social media too."

"I wasn't on social media," she mumbles, reaching up and trapping my hand against her face. "What if I told you I regretted it too?" She lets go and stares intently up at me.

With my free hand I cage her against the counter, still stroking her cheek with my other hand. Her eyes flutter closed as she leans into my touch. I lean closer, rubbing my nose against hers, breathing deeply, drinking her in. Taking a deep breath, I ask, "Can I kiss you?"

I lean back so I can see her when she responds, biting my lip and hoping I didn't screw up my chances.

She opens her eyes. "Yes," she says just loud enough for me to hear.

I send up a silent thanks to whoever or whatever brought her back into my life before brushing my lips against hers in a light kiss. She moans at the contact and grabs the front of my shirt, pulling me closer and kissing me.

I haven't kissed anyone in a very long time. I've certainly never kissed anyone like this. I band my arms around her, pulling her closer. Marveling at how good she tastes, like beer and the pumpkin pie she ate earlier but also like second chances. Weird as that sounds.

I don't know how long we kiss as time seems to both stand still and fly by as we get lost in each other. A throat clearing has me pulling away. I let her go and step back, turning to see Hudson smirking at us.

He raises his eyebrows at me before stepping further into the kitchen and around us to the fridge. I take a deep breath, trying to calm my racing heart, and will my cock to get itself under control.

"Good night." Avery rushes out, breaking the silence as she darts around me and heads for the stairs, her beer forgotten.

I drop my head and grimace. Did I screw that up? She gave me permission to kiss her. Heck, she pulled me in for more.

I sure hope I didn't blow my second chance with her.

Chapter 7

Avery

"Whatcha thinking about?" Caro asks me as we pack our bags the next morning after breakfast with her parents and Hudson.

Thatcher was already gone by the time we went downstairs. Beth said he left early because he had a lot of work to do. So much for getting to see him before we went our separate ways. I'd hoped he would ask for my number or that I'd get a chance to ask him for his. After that kiss we shared last night, I thought he was interested. But I also didn't exactly react in the best possible way.

I freaked out.

His kiss lit me up inside. It made me feel alive. Something I'd never felt before, with Chad or with any of the few boyfriends I'd had before him. Kissing Thatcher felt like a whole otherworldly experience.

But I don't say any of that to Caro. "Not a whole lot. The errands I need to run this weekend."

"Sure. Sure." She takes a seat on the bed and turns to face me. "You're thinking about my twin. Aren't you? Sad that he left without saying goodbye."

I refuse to look at her, instead focusing on shoving my dirty clothes into my overnight bag. "It was fun to see him again. To catch up. But that's all it was. Two old college friends reconnecting."

Caro laughs. "I call bullshit on that. I saw the way you kept shooting glances at each other when we were playing Monopoly. Why do you think I disappeared for so long to put the game away? I figured you two could use some alone time."

"Nothing happened," I mumble, feeling my face heat up. I turn my back to her to gather the rest of my things.

"Oh no you don't." She grabs my arm and tugs on it until I face her. She stares at me for a second, biting her lip. "Something happened, didn't it?"

I stay silent. I'm not answering that question.

"Alright, well, I'm going to do something for you. And him. I hope you both remember this." She lets go of my arm and types something on her phone. "There." She sets it down and gets to her feet. "I sent him a text and asked him if he wants me to give you his number."

"You didn't need to do that, Caro."

"I know I didn't. But I want to see you happy, and if that's him, so be it. Plus, if you can get him to give up his workaholic ways and show up for family events or even just be around more, that would be great too. I miss him." She frowns and I feel bad for monopolizing his time last night. I know everyone was napping but not the entire time.

"So you did this purely for selfish reasons?"

"Maybe." She shrugs.

I shake my head at her, and we finish packing in silence. Downstairs, we say goodbye to her parents and Hudson before heading home.

"Home sweet home," Caro announces when we pull into the parking lot of our complex.

"Thank you for inviting me," I say as we get out of the car.

"Anytime. When we get inside, I'll see if Thatch responded. I still can't believe you and my brother."

"Nothing happened between us."

"But you want something to?"

"I don't know," I answer honestly as we pull our bags out of the trunk.

"Want to talk about it?" she asks as we make our way into our apartment.

"I've been thinking about dating again, but it's a little scary to put myself out there. Dating is so much different now than it was in college." I pause and Caro nods in agreement. "At least I know Thatch already. But what if it doesn't end well between us? I don't want things between you and me to be weird."

"True." Caro clears her throat, studying me for a minute before saying. "I think you should give him a chance and see what happens. It might be awkward at first if things don't work out between you two, but what if it does? You'll never know if you don't try. Know what I mean?"

"I do. And thanks, Caro. I really appreciate it."

"Anytime. Now, I'm going to unpack before I have to get ready for my date."

I head toward my room to unpack as well and figure out how I'm going to spend my Friday evening.

"I texted you Thatch's number. Do you want me to give him yours?" Caro asks a few minutes later from the doorway of my room.

"Yeah, okay."

"What's wrong?" Caro comes into my room and takes a seat at my desk chair.

I sit on the edge of the bed, fiddling with the shirt that I was about to hang up. "I haven't dated anyone in a really long time. Maybe I'm misreading the signs and he just wants to be friends."

"Nah, he's interested. I know my twin."

"I blow out a breath. "I just—" I don't know how to put it into words so she understands what I'm trying to say.

"It's not like you and my brother are running off to get married tomorrow. See where things go." She pauses, glancing around the room. "You're allowed to move on after Chad."

I swallow. How did she know? I don't say that though, instead I give her a weak smile. "I know. I'm nervous." I peer down at the shirt in my lap, afraid to see what her reaction to my omission is.

She puts her hand on top of mine, and I force myself to look up. "It's okay to feel that way, but don't let it stop you from seeing where things go with Thatch. That is, if you want to date him."

"I do."

"Well, good." She gets to her feet. "If he doesn't treat you right, tell me. I'll deal with my little brother. Sound good?"

I snort out a laugh. *Her little brother?* They're twins. "Okay, Caro. Thanks." I stand up and give her a hug. "You're a great friend."

"Now that we got that sorted, I'm going to start some laundry and finish unpacking."

Once she's left my room, I contemplate texting Thatch but chicken out, hoping that he'll text me instead. And if he doesn't, I'll text him.

Tomorrow. Or Sunday.

I grab my current knitting project and head out into the living room, make myself comfortable on the couch, and turn on *Friends*, my comfort show. I lose myself in the repetitive tapping of the knitting needles, counting stitches for who knows how long until Caro walks into the living room, dressed in a pair of dark jeans, a red sweater, and knee-high boots.

"I'm heading out for my date." she announces. "We're meeting at Kobo Bar for drinks. Maybe dinner afterward. We'll see how it goes."

Setting my knitting needles down and pausing *Friends*, I give her my full attention. "You look hot."

"Thanks." She twirls around. "It's the jeans and the boots. What are you up to tonight?"

My stomach chooses that moment to growl loudly. "Maybe I'll go get some sushi."

As soon as I say the words out loud, I know that's exactly what I'll be doing.

"Have fun."

"You too. Text me."

She waves as she heads out the door. I pick up my knitting needles and finish the row that I'm working on. I hate stopping in the middle of a row because I'm always afraid the needle will fall out and I'll lose stitches.

Once that's done, I get ready to go to my favorite sushi restaurant, Akora, in the next town over. I contemplate ordering takeout but that would mean waiting even longer to eat, and I'm too hungry. It's a little after five, but it is a Friday night. I hope it's not too busy. If it is, I'll put in a takeout order or come up with a plan B.

Chapter 8

Thatcher

Groaning, I lean back in my desk chair, tipping my head to stare at the ceiling. I've been trying to figure out this bug for the past three hours and am no closer to a solution. I thought I figured it out an hour ago, but my fix ended up causing a different issue, so I had to revert my changes.

Taking off my glasses, I rub my temple where the beginning of a tension headache is forming. Or maybe it's that I haven't eaten since breakfast.

Shit.

I grab my empty water bottle and head into the kitchen to get a drink and figure out dinner. I don't feel like cooking, and I don't have any leftovers since I was gone the past two days. Sushi it is. I open the junk drawer that doubles as storage for the menus of my favorite restaurants and pull out the one for Akora, a sushi restaurant that I discovered a few weeks ago.

I read the text from my sister with Avery's number in it and contemplate calling her to see if she wants to have dinner. But it's a bit short notice. I'm sure she has plans. Instead, I dial the restaurant and place an order for three rolls—the same ones I had last time. I momentarily consider ordering something different but decide I'd rather not make any more decisions. The woman on the other end of the line tells me it'll be about twenty-five minutes. I thank her and hang up then go back to my computer to save my work before driving over to the restaurant.

Surprisingly there's not a lot of traffic, even though it's a Friday evening, the Friday after Thanksgiving too. I'd expect everyone would be going out to dinner because they're tired of eating leftover turkey. I get to the restaurant early and debate waiting in my car but decide I'd rather go inside, where I can stand after sitting all day.

"Welcome to Akora. How many?" the hostess asks when I step inside the dimly lit restaurant.

"I'm picking up a to go order. For Thatcher."

"Let me go check on that for you, sir." She walks toward the kitchen, and I move out of the way, looking around the dining room.

Sitting in the corner booth, facing the hostess stand and the door, is the woman who I kept thinking about all day and who is probably part of the reason I haven't solved my code issue. I can't stop the grin that spreads across my face when I see her. My feet have a mind of their own, and I find myself walking over to her.

"Hi," I greet Avery as I come to a stop at the end of the table.

"Thatcher. Hey," Avery says, meeting my eyes. "Fancy meeting you here."

"Right? Thought I'd grab an early dinner."

"Me too. Do you want to join me?" she asks, gesturing to the chair across from her.

I really shouldn't. I have work to do tonight, but it's like the universe is purposely putting her in my life.

Again.

And I refuse to screw it up.

Before I can sit down, the hostess walks over. "Sir, your food will be out in another ten minutes. I apologize for the delay."

"Is it too much trouble to change it to a dine in order? Ran into a friend, and I'm going to join her."

"Not at all. I'll let the sushi chef know." She hurries off and I take a seat.

The waitress chooses that moment to come over to the table.

"Hi. The hostess told me that your order is already in. Can I get you anything to drink?" she asks me.

I hesitate for a second, debating whether or not to order something alcoholic. I should order some water because I need to have a clear head to be able to work on my code tonight. But Avery's having a beer. And a beer and sushi sounds good right now. What the heck. "I'll have a Sapporo and a glass of water."

"I'll be right back with that."

"Nice running into you again so soon, Thatch," Avery says before taking a sip of her drink.

"Small world. I didn't know you liked sushi." I internally cringe at that comment.

Really, Thatch? That's all you've got?

She huffs out a laugh. "I didn't always, but then an ex of mine insisted I try one of his sushi rolls one night when we were out on a date. And I didn't hate it. The next time we went out, I ordered my own. The rest is history."

I rest my arms on the table and lean forward. "Want to hear a secret?" I glance around as if to make sure no one is listening.

"Sure."

"I used to only ever order the cooked sushi. Until one time my order got mixed up, and I ended up with a roll that had raw tuna in it. They brought out my correct roll, but I didn't want to let all that fish go to waste. So I tried a piece and realized how much I'd been missing out."

The waitress appears at that moment with our food and I grin when I see we both ordered the same thing.

"Woman after my own heart."

Avery blushes. "It's my favorite so I always order it."

"Me too." We lapse into silence as we eat.

"What are your plans for the weekend?" I ask after we've finished our meals.

"The usual—laundry, grocery shopping, maybe a walk in Grover Park if the weather is nice. There's a new yarn store I want to check out. What about you?"

"Work. Unfortunately."

"Sounds fun."

I shake my head. "Normally I'd say yes, but lately it's been one thing after another. I swear every client project is taking longer than I expected."

"That sucks. Do you just work for other companies? Or do you build your own applications too?"

"Mostly I just do work for other people. It's easier. But I do have one game that's available to the public."

"That's really cool." She pulls her phone out of her purse. "What's it called? I want to download it and play." My chest swells at the fact that Avery not only wants to hear about my business but also support it.

"Let me text you a link to the unlocked version so you won't have to watch ads or pay to unlock more chances." I grab my phone and send her a quick text with the link to the free version.

I move my chair closer to her so I can walk her through a few levels of the game, even though it's pretty self-explanatory. This is the only game I've built that's available to the public. I haven't thought about it in a long time so it's fun to play it again.

"Can I get you anything else?" our waitress asks, reappearing at our table.

"No, thank you. We're all set. We'll take our check whenever."

The waitress nods and disappears. While I'd love to sit here and keep chatting with Avery, I feel bad that we've taken up the table for far longer than necessary.

"You should have asked her for two bills," she says once we're alone again.

"I got it. Want to go for dessert? There's an ice cream shop a few doors down." I know I should get back to work, but I can't make myself. I want to spend more time with her.

"I'm always up for ice cream."

I pay our bill, even though Avery argues, and then we make our way out of the restaurant. I put a hand on the small of her back, guiding her down the sidewalk to the ice cream shop, which is empty too. Guess it pays to eat dinner early.

After getting our order—a waffle cone with a scoop of cookies and cream for Avery and a double scoop of mint chocolate chip in a waffle cone for me—we sit at one of the small tables tucked against the front window of the shop.

Avery takes a bite of her ice cream, moaning as she does. The sound goes straight to my cock, and I adjust myself subtly under the table. Now is not the time nor the place.

"It's good, right?" I ask, taking my own bite and stifling my own groan of appreciation. "They make it here in the shop."

"How did I not know this place was here? I come for sushi at least once a month."

"Maybe because it's so nondescript. I come in this way"—I turn around and gesture to where I enter the shopping plaza—"so I noticed them."

"Do you live close by?"

"I do. About twenty minutes away. Want to come over and watch a movie? Or play a game on Monopoly?" The words are out of my mouth before I can think about them. I hold my breath, hoping she says yes because I desperately want to spend more time with her. As much time as I can. I also hope she doesn't want to play Monopoly because I don't own the game. But I'm sure there's a store nearby where I could buy one if she said she wanted to play.

"I thought you said you had to work," she says with a lift of her eyebrows.

"I do but I've been stuck on a problem for hours. Maybe a night away from it will make it easier to solve."

"That makes sense," she says with a nod. "I'd just hate to get in the way of you getting work done." She takes a bite of her ice cream, and I have to force myself not to stare at the way her tongue peeks out, swiping at the treat.

"I would love to hang out with you," I answer truthfully. Does that make me desperate? Perhaps. At this point, I don't care. I haven't had this much fun in a very long time, and maybe that's exactly what I need.

"If you're sure. All that was on my agenda for the night was to watch TV and knit. But no Monopoly, please. I had my fill at Thanksgiving."

I huff out a laugh. "Noted, no Monopoly."

As I walk her to her car a few minutes later, after we've finished our desserts, I ask, "do you want to follow me? Or I can give you directions?"

"I'll put it in my GPS." She unlocks her sedan and gets in, pulling out her phone.

"Good?" I ask after she's typed in my address.

"Perfect. I'll see you in a few minutes, Thatch."

"Sounds good." I step back so she can close her door. I wait for her to start reversing out of the spot before heading over to my own car and getting in, excited to spend more time with Avery.

Chapter 9

Avery

I can't believe I ran into Thatcher tonight and we had dinner and ice cream together. It felt like a first date but without all the awkwardness. I was secretly cheering when he invited me over to watch a movie. I didn't want our time together tonight to end.

I force myself to focus on the road, and a short while later, I'm pulling up to his building.

Once I'm parked, I text Caro to let her know where I am so she doesn't worry when she gets home. As I'm putting my phone back in my purse, Thatch walks over to my car.

"Find it alright?" he asks by way of greeting when I get out.

"Yep." I swallow, trying to shove down the nerves that are threatening to make an appearance.

"I'm this way." He points at the building in front of us.

I follow him to his apartment and wait while he inputs the code to unlock the door. We take our shoes off, and then he guides me into the living room, a hand on my lower back. I love that he does that. Or maybe I just like that he's touching me.

"Make yourself at home." He gestures to a worn but comfortable-looking couch against one wall of the room with a dark-blue blanket draped over one side and two matching pillows haphazardly thrown on one end. "Do you want something to drink? Beer? Water? I don't think I've got anything else besides that. Maybe some random tea. Oh, coffee, I do have coffee, but not sure if you want to drink that late at night." He huffs out a laugh, clearly nervous, which makes me less nervous.

"Water is fine. Thanks," I say, taking a seat on one end of the couch.

He leaves to get our drinks, and I take in the rest of the living room. On each side of the couch are dark-brown side tables bare of anything except coasters and a lamp. A matching coffee table, holding only another coaster and a remote, sits close enough that I can put my feet up on it. An entertainment console, with a few picture frames and an Xbox sitting on top, and a rather large wall-mounted television take up most of the opposite wall.

Either Thatcher is a minimalist, or he's never gotten around to decorating. Regardless, I like the simplicity. It's probably easy to clean since there aren't a lot of knickknacks on all the surfaces like there are at mine and Caro's place.

The room is cozy and comfortable even if the walls are bare. Not that I blame him. If this is a rental, putting anything up means having to patch and possibly touch up paint when you move. Something I'd rather avoid as well.

"Here you go." Thatch makes his way over to me and hands me a glass of water. "Any idea what movie we should watch?"

"No. Not really." I take the offered glass and set it on a coaster on the side table.

"I don't even know what's out. Can't tell you the last time I sat down and watched a movie or even a television show. I've been so busy."

Oh.

"Are you sure you can take time off tonight? I don't want to cause you to miss a deadline or be even more stressed out." Maybe I should go. Leave Thatcher to work.

"Don't go." He puts a hand on my arm, and my skin heats at his touch. "Please. I want to spend time with you."

"Okay." I lean back against the couch cushions. He moves his hand, and I miss his touch.

"What do you like to watch?" He picks up the remote.

"I usually watch *Friends* when I knit." I shrug. "It's my comfort show, so I don't have to fully pay attention to it since I've seen it so many times. Occasionally, I'll watch *Survivor* or whatever random reality show Caro is watching."

"I've never seen *Friends*."

"What?" I stare at him, flabbergasted.

He gives me a boyish grin, his dimples peeking out, and I swoon.

"I was always too busy doing schoolwork or working to have much time for television. When I do have downtime, I usually game." He gestures to his Xbox. "Let's watch it. You might have to fill me in on things though."

He hands me the remote, and I navigate to the show, deciding to start with the pilot so he can get the full experience. At some point we shift closer to each other, so our thighs touch, and he wraps his arm around me, pulling me into him.

I don't know if it's the beer I had with dinner or the warmth of his embrace, but my eyes grow heavy, and I drift off to sleep leaning against him.

I startle awake when Shadow jumps onto my lap.

"Hi, kitty."

He purrs and lets me pet him a couple of times before he pads across my legs and into the spot next to me. The *empty* spot next to me. I squint, glancing around the dark room, the television off, looking for Thatcher. Maybe he went to the bathroom. I lift my arms above my head, stretching my neck to work out the kink that's formed. I reach over and turn the lamp on, blinking at the sudden light, and wait for my eyes to adjust.

I walk out of the living room and peek my head into the kitchen, which is also empty.

"Thatch," I call as I walk down the hallway toward the only room with a light on. I come to a halt in the doorway of what I assume is his office.

"Avery," he says, spinning around in his chair, computer screens lit up behind him.

"Why didn't you wake me?"

"I was going to in a little bit." He glances at his computer, frowning. "Time got away from me. I figured out the bug I was stuck on earlier."

"That's good." He's not Chad, I remind myself. Just because he went back to work tonight while I was over does not mean he's my ex. Thatch said he's been trying to figure this issue out all day. I lean against the doorframe, yawning. "What time is it?"

"After midnight." He turns back to his computer, clicks a few buttons before shutting off the screens, and standing up. "Do you want to stay?" he asks, shuffling back and forth, his hands shoved in his pockets. "I'll sleep on the couch, and you can take my bed."

"I can't do that. I'll go home. It's fine." I yawn again.

"I won't force you to stay, Avery, but it's late, and it's a long drive. That being said, I understand if you aren't comfortable with it."

I smile up at him, butterflies taking flight at his words. It's not even the fact that he cares about me that much, but that he understands I might not want to sleep over. Chad would never have done that. He would have told me that I was staying.

"I'll stay. I don't really want to drive this late. But we can share the bed, or I'll sleep on the couch. There's no way you'll be comfortable on it. I don't mind."

Thatch studies me for a few beats before extending his hand. "We can share the bed if you're sure."

I nod.

He wraps his fingers around mine. "Come on. I'll find you a spare toothbrush."

He leads me to the bathroom and gets me a toothbrush still in its packaging from under the sink and hands me a clean towel from the linen closet.

"I'll find you something to sleep in too," he says before stepping out and closing the door.

I take my time brushing my teeth, washing my face, and using the toilet. I free my hair from the bun it's been in all day, letting it fall across my shoulders. I'll probably wake up with it knotted, but it's more comfortable when it's down. Opening the door, I leave the light on for Thatch and walk toward his room.

"Can I come in?" I ask, pausing at the doorway.

"Yeah."

I step in and look around. It's decorated much the same as the living room, with dark-brown furniture and a matching navy-blue comforter. "You really like blue."

He smirks, glancing around. "I do. It also hides the cat hair." I chuckle.

"Here." He hands me a shirt and pair of boxers. "Found you something to wear. I'm going to use the bathroom."

I slowly peel off my sweater, socks, and jeans and replace them with the clothes he gave me, which smell like him. I debate for a minute about whether to leave my bra on or take it off and ultimately decide I'd rather not sleep with it on.

I set my folded clothes on top of his dresser, which is devoid of anything except a framed photo of him and his siblings—the same one Caro has at our apartment. I climb into bed, choosing the spot farthest away from the door and hoping that it isn't the side he prefers.

A few minutes later, he walks back into the room, having swapped his jeans for a pair of black athletic shorts. Standing in front of the bed, he takes off his glasses and sets them on the nightstand next to his phone before pulling off his shirt. I know I shouldn't stare, but I can't help it.

I sigh.

Thatch definitely spends time at the gym. Based on the muscles in his shoulders and his arms, *plenty* of time. He grins at me. He must have heard me. My gaze travels down the length of his chest, which is as muscular and magnificent as I pictured.

"Like what you see?" he asks as he moves the covers and lies down next to me.

My face heats up at being called out. But you know what, who cares? He clearly likes me based on the kiss we shared the other night and the fact that we spent the evening together.

"Yes," I answer honestly.

His eyes widen and his smirk turns into a full-blown smile, his dimples making an appearance. "Good."

He shifts closer and gives me the quickest kiss on the lips before pulling back and reaching over to turn off the light. "Does that mean you want to go out on a third date with me?"

"Yes, but third? Besides tonight, when was our other date?"

"Thanksgiving in my parents' sunroom was our first date. Tonight was most definitely our second. Good night, Avery."

"Night, Thatch."

I close my eyes, taking a few deep breaths. I really want to move closer to him and kiss him again, do more, but I get the sense that he wants to go slow.

Is that for my benefit?

Or his?

Why is someone massaging my back?

I jolt awake and scare Shadow, who was apparently walking on me. He moves to the foot of the bed where he sits and glares at me.

Yes, Shadow glares at me. Probably wondering why his side of the bed is taken up.

I take a few deep breaths to calm my racing heart. That's one way to wake up. Thatcher's breathing is even, indicating that he's still asleep. I run a hand down my face, replaying the events of last night. In the light of day, I feel silly for staying over.

What does that say about me? Sleeping with a guy after a second date? Although it's not like we did anything except sleep.

Regardless, I should probably go home. I'm grateful Thatcher's still asleep, so I don't have to deal with the awkward morning after. If that makes me a coward, so be it.

Taking a deep breath, I creep out of bed, grab my clothes, and make my way into the bathroom. I quickly change, brush my teeth, and run my fingers through my hair and put it in a messy bun. I tiptoe to the kitchen where I find a piece of paper and a pen and scribble a note.

That done, I grab my purse from by the door, put my shoes on, and head out, locking up behind me using the keypad.

It's early for a Saturday morning, which means there's hardly any traffic, and I make it home quickly.

"Well, look who finally decided to come home," Caro says with a grin from the couch, where she's curled up with a blanket, when I walk in the apartment.

"Did you fall asleep on the couch again?"

"Yeah. I was watching reruns of *Survivor*, waiting for you to come home. I woke up a few times, but I was too tired to move." She stretches, patting the spot next to her.

"I'm sorry," I say, feeling guilty for not telling her I wasn't coming home.

"It's fine," she says with a wave of her hand as I take a seat. "Have fun with Thatch?" She smirks at me.

"We watched *Friends*. Fell asleep, and he asked me to stay over." I omit the part where I woke up on the couch alone and found him working in his office.

"Oh." She bounces her eyebrows at me. "Anything happen?"

I start to answer, but before I can, she puts up a hand. "Wait, I don't want the details. That's my brother."

I throw back my head, laughing. "Nothing happened."

"He must really like you."

"Why?" I ask, furrowing my brows.

"Because he watched TV with you instead of working."

"Oh." Should I tell her the truth? I don't want her to get mad at Thatch on my behalf. I do understand why he did what he did.

"No. No." Caro waves her hand at me. "None of that. He's an adult. He can make his own decisions."

"I know." I stare down at my hands in my lap, picking at the seam of my shirt. "I feel a little silly for staying over last night. We've only just started seeing each other." I glance up at my friend to find her studying me.

"You're both adults. There's no set timeline for what happens when."

"True." I agree before changing the subject. "How was your date?" She makes a face. "That good, eh?"

"Another bust." She throws her hands up. "I barely made it through drinks with him. All he wanted to do was talk about himself and his job. I told him I felt a migraine coming on when he suggested dinner."

"Maybe you do need to try to meet a guy the old-fashioned way instead of on an app." I wave my hand at her phone, which is in her lap.

"Maybe."

I get to my feet, knowing not to push the subject. "I'm going to go shower and change. How about we go out for brunch?"

"Sounds good."

I walk out of the room, replaying everything that happened between Thatch and I last night. It was a good night. I enjoy spending time with him. I hope I didn't screw things up leaving like I did this morning.

Chapter 10

Thatcher

Shadow's meowing wakes me up, and I open my eyes to see him sitting on the pillow next to me.

"Could you do that somewhere else?" I ask him when he sprawls out and starts to lick himself. He glances up at me for a second as if to consider my question before going back to his bath.

Shaking my head at my cat, I sit up and grab my glasses. If Shadow is in here, where's Avery?

"Avery?" I call, getting out of bed and walking into the hallway. The bathroom door is open, so I know she's not in there. Nor is she in the living room. In the kitchen, I spot a note propped up against the coffee pot.

Thatch,

Thanks for a great time last night and for letting me crash in your bed. I have a bunch of errands and chores, and I know you have work to do. Talk soon.

Avery

I groan, running a hand through my hair. Did I screw something up? I think through the events of last night. Was she mad that I was working while she was asleep on the couch? Maybe that wasn't a good idea, but the solution to the issue I was having suddenly dawned on me, and I knew if I didn't get up to try it, I'd end up forgetting it.

She said she understood. We kissed goodnight. Everything seemed fine when we went to bed. Maybe it is like her note says, and she has a lot to do. Regardless, I don't have time to dwell on it. I do have work to do. A lot of it since I didn't get as much done last night as I'd planned to.

"Worth it," I mumble as I make my way to my bathroom to shower and get ready for a day full of sitting in front of my computer.

A couple of hours later, I find myself yet again replaying last night's events over and over and not focusing on the code in front of me. I decide to call my sister to see if she knows anything.

"Hey," Caro says, answering on the first ring.

"Hi."

"Heard you had a sleepover last night."

"I did. But now I'm afraid I screwed it up with her. Nothing even happened. I just . . ." I trail off, pacing my living room, running a hand through my hair.

"Calm down, little brother. From what Avery said, she had a good time. I think she's a little scared."

"Why is she scared?" I ask, coming to a halt, my heart racing. Did I do something wrong? I don't think I did. I thought I was respectful and polite, even though all I really wanted to do was kiss her senseless.

"You're the first guy she's dated since her divorce. I'm sure that's scary."

"Okay." I breathe out a sigh of relief. I can understand that. It's been a long time since I've dated too, even longer since I've been in a relationship. "What can I do?"

"Woo her, Thatch. I don't think she's had that. Be patient with her."

I nod, even though my sister can't see me. "I can do that."

"You like her a lot?" she asks, and I can hear the happiness in her voice.

"I do," I admit. "And now I have a second chance to date her, and I'm taking it."

"Good. Well, I've got to go, we're going grocery shopping."

"Thanks, sis."

"You're welcome, little brother."

I shake my head, hanging up the phone. Woo her, Caroline said. That's exactly what I'm going to do.

I open my internet browser, pull up the website for a local florist, and place an order for a gorgeous vase full of assorted flowers to be delivered tomorrow morning. That done, I get up to make myself a second cup of coffee before going back to work.

A few hours later, I stand, stretching, and walk into the kitchen for some more water and a snack. I decide to text Avery.

Me:

> Hey. I had a lot of fun last night. Hope I can see you again soon.

I reread the text message a couple of times, agonizing over whether I should say something else, before finally hitting send.

When I'm cleaning up after lunch, my phone vibrates. I grab it, hoping it's Avery, but it's Anders, my best friend.

Want to meet at the gym at four for a workout?

I contemplate telling him no, but he'd just show up at my door and force me to go anyway—he's only asking to be polite. I send him a thumbs up and get back to work, determined to make the most of the next three hours.

"Thatch, are you even paying attention?" Anders asks. I stare blankly at him. He shakes his head. "You were ten minutes late, and now you're in another world." He waves a hand at me. "Coding issues still?"

"Yes." I grab my water bottle, taking a drink from it before telling him about Thanksgiving and Avery.

"*The* Avery Butler? As in Avery who you had a crush on and almost went out on a date with until the hurricane spoiled your plans?" he asks as we put weights on the bar for chest presses.

I laugh. "Yeah, her."

Anders and I were roommates, so he knows what went down and how much I agonized over our canceled date.

"Dude. That's fate. I think it was meant to be. After all these years. You're single. She's single."

I blow out a breath as I lie down on the bench, situating my hands on the bar. I don't say anything as I complete a set of chest presses. I set the bar down and sit up, wiping my hands on my towel before standing.

"I guess. I just have so much to do right now." I run the towel over my face. "It's frustrating because all I want to do is spend time with her, and I have to work." I scrunch up my face as I speak.

"I keep telling you to hire someone to help you," Anders says as he takes my spot on the bench.

"I know. I know." I rake a hand through my damp hair.

He meets my eyes, his face turning serious. "As your accountant, I'm telling you that you can afford to. You'd still be in charge. It won't be like last time . . ." He lets the rest go unsaid as he starts his set, but I know what he means.

It won't be like the last time, when my business partner, Nigel, didn't do any of the work he was supposed to, and we fell so far behind that the application we'd been contracted to build never got finished.

Our company folded because we had to pay back the retainer as per our contract. The money had already been spent on setting up a small office space and Nigel disappeared without a trace so I repaid the money from my savings. When I finally got a hold of him, he said he'd pay me back half but he never did.

I thought Nigel was a safe bet because I'd known him from college. We'd worked our first job together, and he was a great employee, constantly getting praise from managers, so I'd assumed he was a good pick for a business partner. Clearly, I was wrong. I had to take a corporate job because I needed the steady income.

When I finally started Wells Tech, I swore I'd never put myself or my company in that position again. "I'll think about it," I finally say ten minutes later as we're unracking the bar.

Anders stares at me for a few seconds, and I brace myself for what he's going to say.

"I want you to be happy, Thatch. I've watched you work so hard for the past couple of years on growing your client base and building your business's reputation. I know you've got a lot of projects coming in. More than one person can handle. You can't lock yourself away in your apartment and work twenty-four seven, it's not healthy."

"I know, Anders. I know." I look down at the floor, collecting my thoughts before meeting his eyes. "It's hard to trust anyone to do a good job."

He claps me on the back. "I know. But you need to. Come on, let's finish up our workout so you can get back to your code or your new girlfriend." He wiggles his eyebrows at me, and I shove his shoulder as we walk toward the free weight section of the gym.

A few hours later, freshly showered and having eaten dinner, I sit down at my computer in my office. But I can't focus. Instead, my thoughts go to Avery, to the past few days, and finally to what Anders said about hiring help. It would be nice not to have to do everything by myself. But it would also mean trusting someone with my baby. I'm not sure if I can do that. Not after what happened the last time.

I force myself to concentrate on the screen in front of me, and when I finally come up for air, it's past midnight. I stand, stretching my stiff muscles. Where did the whole evening go? At least I got all the code done. Now I have to do a final check and test everything. Opening the top drawer of my desk, I pull out my phone to see I have a missed text from Avery.

Avery:

I had a lot of fun too. Would love to see you again. Let me know when you're free.

I start to type a response, but since it's so late, I probably shouldn't. I lock my phone, making a mental note to respond in the morning, and head out of my office to find something to eat.

Chapter 11

Avery

"Avery, there's a delivery for you," Caro calls from the living room.

A delivery? For me? On a Sunday. Putting down the shirt I was in the middle of hanging up, I walk out of my bedroom. My steps falter as I spot the vase of flowers in Caro's hand.

She hands it to me. "These came for you."

"Oh." I bring the assortment of daisies, sunflowers, and other colorful flowers I can't identify to my nose, inhaling their sweet scent.

"There's a card." She points to it. "But I'm sure we can guess who they're from."

"They could be from my parents," I say, walking into the kitchen and setting the vase down before grabbing the card. My lips tip up into a grin as I read:

Avery,

I'm so glad you're back in my life. I had a great time with you on Friday. Can't wait to take you out for a third date soon.

Yours

Thatcher.

"What does it say?"

I hand it to her, staring at the flowers. I can't believe Thatch sent me them.

"I can't remember the last time anyone got me flowers." I pause, racking my brain. "Oh wait, my parents sent me some when my divorce was final."

"He likes you a lot."

I blush. "I'm going to go call him." I scoop up the vase and card, walk to my room, and set them on my nightstand. Pushing my abandoned clean laundry to one side of the bed, I sit down and call Thatch.

"Hey, sunshine." He greets me on the first ring.

"Hey, Mr. Romantic."

He chuckles, a deep sound that makes my body shiver with anticipation. "I take it you got the flowers."

"I did. Thank you. They're beautiful."

"You're welcome. Does that mean we're still on for a third date?"

"Of course it does."

He clears his throat. "Good. I'm glad. I wasn't sure after Saturday morning. I was afraid I came on too strong."

"No. You didn't. I'm sorry I freaked out and left without saying goodbye. I'm not good at this whole dating thing."

"Was it too much too soon?" he asks quietly.

"No," I answer without a second's hesitation.

"Good."

We lapse into silence. But not an awkward silence, a comfortable one.

"What are you up to today?" I ask, crossing my fingers that maybe we can see each other again, even though I saw him only a little over twenty-four hours ago.

He sighs. "Working all day."

"How's it going?"

"I got a lot done yesterday. Started testing the code, and so far, everything's going smoothly. Hopefully I can wrap this up today so I can start on my next project."

"Anything I can do to help?" I don't know why I'm asking. It's not like I know anything about software development.

"Nah. I appreciate it though. It's going to be a long day."

"I hope it goes well."

We chat for a few more minutes before he says he needs to get back to work.

I'm pulling into the parking lot in front of my apartment complex on Wednesday evening when my phone rings.

"Hey, Thatch." We've texted a few times the past couple of days, but this is the first time we've talked since Sunday morning.

"Hey, sunshine. What are you doing on Saturday evening?"

"Nothing. Why? What's up?"

"Want to go to a hockey game with me?"

I perk up. He wants to take me to a hockey game?

"Yes," I say a little too loudly.

"I was hoping you'd say that. I got us ice-level seats for the Wings Storm game. I picked seats where the Storm attack twice."

I'm speechless. How'd he get those tickets? And on the glass? Or that's what I assume he means by ice-level seats.

"Seriously, Thatch?"

"Yeah, you said you liked the Storm, and I saw they were in town, so . . ."

"I'd love to go with you," I say, grinning. I know he can't see me, but I hope he can hear the excitement in my voice.

"How about I pick you up since we have to go that way anyway to get to the arena?"

"Sure, that works."

"Do you want to stay over after? I'll drive you home on Sunday."

"I'd like that."

"Good." I hear a beeping in the background. "Shit. Sorry. Dinner's ready. Can I call you later, so we can work out the details?"

"That works. I just got home anyway and need to find something to eat."

"Okay. Bye."

I hang up the phone and hurry into the apartment, where I'm greeted by the aroma of freshly baked cookies. Uh-oh. Caro's had a bad day. When she's upset or stressed, she bakes.

"You alright, Caro?" I ask, slipping off my shoes and setting my laptop bag on the couch before making my way into the kitchen.

"Yep. Yep," Caro says as she bends down to pull a cookie sheet from the oven before turning it off.

"I'm calling BS." I glance around the kitchen that's covered in plates and trays of cookies. Definitely not doing good.

"Fine. You're right," she says, whirling around to face me, oven mitts on her hands.

I try and fail not to wince at the state of her. Her Kiss the Cook apron is covered in flour and chocolate, her face has smudges of flour on it, even her hair, tied in a messy bun, has flour in it.

"What can I do?" I ask, taking the oven mitts off her hands. "Maybe you should sit down." I point to the kitchen table before filling two glasses with water.

Chances are she hasn't had enough to drink or eat today. First order of business is to get her hydrated and fed.

"Here." I place the glass of water in front of her on the table before taking a seat. "Drink and then talk to me."

She lifts her head off the table and does as I tell her.

After a few minutes of silence, she asks, "What happens if I never find my person?"

Woah. Did not see that one coming. I take a sip of water, contemplating her question.

"Where'd this come from?"

She seemed fine this morning when I left for work. If she hadn't, I would have worked from home so I could be here for her.

She runs a hand down her face. "I deleted the dating apps on my phone. My parents were right, using them wasn't getting me anywhere. Then I got to thinking, how am I going to meet someone without them? I feel like I'm running out of time." The last part comes out in a whisper.

"Ilsy," I say, taking her hand in mine. "Just because you're single in your mid-thirties does not mean you're running out of time."

She stares down at our clasped hands. "I spiraled this afternoon and started baking." She takes a shaky breath. "I'm sorry. I don't know why I let that bad date on Friday go to my head. Maybe because I'm seeing you and my brother start dating. He's buying you flowers and making you smile more. I realized how much I want that."

"I'm sorry." Shit. I didn't mean to make her feel bad.

"No. No. It's nothing either of you did. It's all on me. I want you to be happy. Thatch too. I always wanted a sister. I'm glad you found each other again. Maybe one day that'll happen to me."

"I'm sure your person is out there. And don't rush into calling me your sister that quickly. Thatch and I are still super new, and I'm the one with a failed marriage under my belt."

"That wasn't your fault. Chad's a jackass and didn't see what he had in front of him. But I'm kind of thankful because it gave me you." She glances around the kitchen. "We probably shouldn't eat cookies for dinner, eh?"

"Probably not." I walk over to the fridge to see what we can have for dinner.

"Want to take some cookies to the office tomorrow?"

"Sure." I survey the contents of the fridge, trying to figure out what's quick and easy. "How does stir fry sound?"

"Perfect."

I run to my room to change while Caro gets started cleaning up the kitchen so we can cook.

Forty-five minutes later, as we're eating, I tell her about Thatcher inviting me to a hockey game this weekend.

"Wait a minute." She sets her fork down and stares at me. "You're telling me that my brother bought tickets to a professional hockey game?"

"Yes."

"Thatch doesn't watch sports. Never has. I couldn't even talk him into going to our school's football games with me when we were in high school."

I laugh, shrugging my shoulders and continuing to eat.

"The man has it bad."

"He bought tickets on the glass too. For the side the Storm attack twice."

Caro crinkles her forehead. "I don't even know what that means, and I'm sure he doesn't either." She pauses, meeting my gaze. "Which means he looked it all up. Probably called Anders." She rolls her eyes. Why, I don't know. "And had him help find tickets."

"Who's Anders?"

"That's what you got from that? Not the fact that Thatch went through all that trouble for you."

I point my fork at her. "I know how much trouble he went through. What I'm more curious about is who Anders is and why mentioning him causes you to roll your eyes."

She rolls her eyes again. "He's Thatch's BFF. They went to college together. Heck, I'm shocked you don't know him. They were roommates."

"Thatch and I had a couple of classes together and were in the same study group. We didn't interact much outside of that. Maybe if we had gone out on a date. But we didn't, so I never met his friends."

"Well, Anders is Mr. Uptight CPA Accountant. I swear the man irons his underwear. He probably doesn't know how to have a good time."

I snort out a laugh. "And you would know how?"

"A feeling I get. Everything about him is always so neat and particular. I swear the man never has a hair out of place. I wonder how much time he spends getting ready every morning."

"Sounds like you're very interested in what he does and doesn't do every morning."

"Am not. I'm stating facts."

"And you don't like him because he's so put together?"

She takes a bite of stir fry, chews, and swallows. "We've never gotten along. We're like oil and water."

I crinkle my forehead but don't ask any more questions, even though I have a feeling there's more to the story than she's telling me. We start talking about other things, but I can't help but mull over what Caroline said about how much effort Thatcher put into getting tickets to the hockey game.

For me.

Not because he's a fan. But because he heard me when I told him I loved hockey and the Storm.

It makes my heart swell, and if I wasn't already falling for him, I definitely would be now.

Chapter 12

Thatcher

I glance at the clock in my car for the fifth time, cursing myself for running half an hour late, even though I set five different alarms and reminders on my phone and laptop.

I texted Avery when I was leaving my place and knew I wouldn't make it on time. Her response was that it was fine and to drive safely. I just hope it *is* fine and she's not mad.

It's my own fault. I knew I needed to stop working, but I was almost done with the section of code I was writing, so I kept going.

I'm crossing my fingers it doesn't take as long as Anders said it would to park and that we still get there early enough to get food and watch warm-ups. Because according to him, Avery will want to watch them. I didn't even realize that was a thing.

I wanted everything to be perfect for tonight. I had a whole plan in place, but I blew it.

I've never put this much effort into a date, but there's something about Avery that makes me want to go above and beyond for her. Show her she's the most important person in my life. Even if she's only been back in it for a couple of weeks. Call me crazy, but it is what it is.

Thankfully, the universe hears at least some of my pleas because the drive from my place to Avery's is quick, and I arrive a few minutes earlier than I expected.

"Hey, little bro." Caro greets me at the door, holding it open so I can step inside.

"Hey, Caro," I say, giving her a hug.

"She'll be right out," she says as we walk into the kitchen, leaning against the counter and crossing her arms. "She's super excited for tonight. She hasn't stopped talking about it."

"Good, I'm glad." I shove my hands in my pockets, glancing around the room to avoid my sister's nosy gaze.

Before either of us can say anything else, Avery walks into the room, and I lose my ability to breathe. She's gorgeous. Somehow more so than the other times I've seen her.

She's wearing dark wash jeans, a pair of black sneakers, and, based on the cloud and lightning logo on the front of it, a long-sleeve Storm jersey. Yes, I did my research about the team last night and tried my best to memorize the basics. Her brown hair is loose in waves down her back.

"Hi," she says, stepping up to me, and I wrap my arms around her, pulling her in tight to my chest.

She tips her head up to look at me, and I hesitate for a second, wondering if I should kiss her or not. Are we at that stage? She answers that query for me when she leans up and briefly brushes her lips against mine.

"Not so fast," I whisper.

I lean down and seal our lips together in what I intended to be a quick kiss, but at the taste of her I get lost, kissing her deeper and running my tongue along the seam of her mouth. She opens for me, and I swipe my tongue inside.

A throat clearing has us stopping all too quickly. Avery chuckles as she steps out of my embrace.

"Alright, kids. You have a good time now," Caro says with a smirk.

I shake my head at her, and she winks.

"Ready?" I ask Avery.

"Almost, I have to get my bag, but I wanted to say hi to you first."

I nod as she hurries out of the room.

"What?" I ask my sister, catching her staring at me.

She shrugs. "Happy for you two."

Avery returns to the kitchen with an overnight bag slung over her shoulder, which I take from her, as well as a small purse thing, her jacket, and a scarf in the same colors and with the same logo as her jersey.

"Here." She offers the scarf to me.

"Is this not okay?" I ask, glancing down at the jeans and navy-blue sweatshirt I picked out. I looked up the Storm's colors so I could figure out what to wear. I got lucky that their colors make up the majority of my wardrobe.

"No, you look good. I grabbed it in case you wanted to wear something with their logo on it." She moves to put it around her neck.

"I'll wear it." I put my hand out for the scarf.

Avery hugs Caro goodbye, and they whisper together for a couple of seconds, likely about me because they keep glancing over in my direction. Finally, we're out the door.

"I'm sorry I was late," I tell her when we're in my car.

"It's fine, Thatch."

I lean back against the headrest, closing my eyes for a second. "It's not fine. I knew I needed to leave to come pick you up, and I didn't."

"But you're here now, and that's all that matters."

"Okay." I heave out a breath. "Let's go watch some hockey." I put the car into reverse and head toward the highway.

"I'm so excited for tonight. Did I ever say thank you for this?" Avery asks, turning in her seat when we stop at a stoplight.

"You did." I smile at her, squeezing her hand before focusing on the road. "But you can say it again. I'm glad you're excited. I am too. I've never been to a hockey game."

We chat about our weeks, and she tells me about a new client she's working on a marketing plan for as I drive toward the stadium. As we get closer to our destination, the amount of traffic increases.

Shit, Anders wasn't kidding.

"I'm kind of shocked at how many people are going to the same place as we are." There's a long line of cars in front of and behind us, all waiting to turn into the street where the parking garage is. "Good thing I prepaid for parking."

"I had a feeling it was going to be this way. The Storm won the Stanley Cup last year, so I figured everyone would want to come and see them play."

"Oh." Thank goodness I also did a deep dive on the NHL last night when I was researching the Storm, so I can appreciate what winning the Stanley Cup means. "You're probably going to have to explain what's going on during the game. I looked up the basics, but things like icing and offsides made no sense to me. I think I understand power plays and the different types of penalties though."

Avery shakes her head. "I've been watching hockey since I was a kid, and even *I* don't totally understand offsides or icing every time. Seems like it depends on who the refs are and how they're feeling that particular day."

I chuckle, relieved to hear that I won't be alone in not understanding every nuance of the game.

After another fifteen minutes of stop-and-go traffic, we finally turn into the parking garage and find a place to park. Going through security is a quick process, as is getting our tickets scanned at the door.

Avery glances at one of the televisions mounted on the wall on the concourse.

"They're already warming up," she says, frowning.

Fuck.

If I didn't feel shitty before, I do now. I hope I can make it up to her.

"Let's go watch. Then we can find some food." I take her hand, and after consulting the tickets on my phone, I locate our section, and soon, we're walking down the stairs to our seats.

"This is awesome," she says once we're seated.

We get to watch the last few minutes of warm-ups. When the players disappear down the tunnel to their locker rooms, we head up to the main concourse to find something to eat for dinner.

I spend most of the next couple of hours alternating between watching Avery as she cheers and yells for her team and watching the game. I never really thought about how much skill it takes to be a hockey player until I was sitting up close, watching them as they skated around the ice effortlessly, passing pucks and hitting each other into the boards.

It ends up being a lot of fun, and I find myself yelling for the Storm players to shoot the puck or skate away from a Wings player.

"That's Hunter Rhodes," Avery says, pointing to a player who currently has the puck and is being pursued by not one, but two Wings players. "He's only been playing professionally for a few seasons now."

I smile and nod, all the while wanting to pull her into my arms and kiss her senseless.

When the game is over, with the Storm winning four to two, we walk hand in hand out to the parking garage.

"Thank you again, Thatch." Avery turns to me as we come to a stop next to the passenger side of my car.

"You don't have to keep thanking me. I had a lot of fun too."

She chews on her bottom lip, and I can't help myself. I know we're in public, but I step closer to her and capture her lips in a deep, rough kiss. She grips the front of my sweatshirt, pulling me closer to her. Her tongue swipes against my mouth, and I open for her. Banding my arms around her, I hold her close, enjoying the way she tastes, the way she feels against me. Eventually I pull away, even though I don't want to. We are in the middle of the parking garage after all. The gorgeous woman in front of me is breathtaking, her cheeks flushed from our make out session, and her pupils blown wide with desire.

All for me.

"You're killing me," I mumble, kissing her cheek.

"How long will it take to get to your place?" she asks, trailing her hand down my body and over my hard, aching cock. I thrust into her. Wanting more. Wanting her to wrap her hands around me and make me come.

"Too long." I press my forehead against hers and take a deep breath. "But it'll take even longer if we don't get a move on."

She giggles, turning to open the passenger side door, and I can't help but gently smack her ass. She glances at me over her shoulder, smirking. I shake my head and help her into the car.

Closing her door, I discreetly adjust myself, thankful for the low lighting, and make my way around to my side to get in.

The game might have been fun, but I have a feeling the night is about to get even better.

Chapter 13

Avery

Thatcher's kisses lit a fire inside of me, one that I haven't felt in a long time, perhaps not ever, and one that I somehow know won't be put out until he's buried deep inside of me bringing me to orgasm. I clench my legs together, trying to gain some relief. My underwear is ruined, and all he did was kiss me. I suppose the whole feeling him hard for me from our kisses added to it. The thought of him hard makes me shiver.

"You okay? Want to turn the heat on?"

"I'm good." My voice comes out husky and needy and I turn to gaze out the window, hoping to distract myself.

He chuckles, a deep, throaty rumble that hits me low in the stomach and makes me ache for him even more.

"Don't do that," I mumble.

"Do what?"

"Laugh all sexy like. It's not helping." I cross my arms over my chest

"I'm sorry." He looks over at me for a second, but it's too dark for me to read his expression.

"It's fine." I flash him a grin before reaching over to fiddle with the radio, finally settling on a station that's playing pop rock.

I think back through the events of the night. It's been way too long since I've been to a hockey game. I forgot how much I loved being at one. I was a little frustrated that we missed most of warm-ups, but I'm choosing to not dwell on that and instead focus on all the things that went perfectly.

When we finally pull into a parking space in front of his apartment, he unbuckles his seatbelt and says, "Stay there."

Before I can respond, he's out of the car and around to my side, opening my door and helping me out. He holds my hand as we grab my bag from the trunk and rush into his apartment.

The minute the front door is closed and locked, he cages me against the wall with his hands. He leans down and kisses me, gripping my hip. A whimper escapes me, and I grab his sweatshirt, pulling him closer. His tongue swipes against my lips, and I open for him. My center aches, and I grind against him, eliciting a moan from him that makes me even more needy for his touch.

He breaks off our kiss, letting go of my hip and taking a half step back. I immediately miss him. He stares at me, his lips swollen, chest heaving.

"I can't help myself around you, Avery. You're addicting."

I giggle, taking his hand and tugging him further into the apartment. I'm on a mission.

"Where are we going, sunshine?"

I glance over my shoulder at him. "Somewhere more comfortable." I sit down on the couch, patting the cushion next to me. He complies, but surprises me when he pulls me into his lap. My eyes flutter shut when I feel him hard against my core.

"Feel what you do to me," Thatcher rasps out, thrusting against me.

I groan. "Thatch."

"Yes?" He leans forward and kisses me again. I wrap my arms around him as I kiss him back.

We get lost in each other for a few minutes before he says, "Do you want to go to my room? Take these clothes off?"

I take a deep breath, trying to collect my thoughts. I want him, and he clearly wants me. But is it too soon?

"Talk to me. What's going on in your head?" Thatch whispers.

"Are we rushing into things?" I ask, too nervous to look him in the eyes.

"Hey, look at me." Thatch tips my chin up, so I have no choice but to do what he says. "I won't push you to do anything you're not ready for. We can turn on a movie or *Friends* and cuddle on the couch. We can take this relationship however slow you want. I'm not in a hurry. I'm happy just being with you."

"Is that what this is? A relationship?"

Thatch shrugs. "We don't have to put a title on what we are, but I have no interest in dating any other woman. You're the only one I want."

"I don't want to date anyone else either," I admit. I've been falling for Thatcher since we kissed on Thanksgiving.

"Good." He leans forward and gives me a chaste kiss. "Girlfriend."

"Okay, boyfriend," I answer, leaning closer and kissing him back. Pulling away, I stare up at him for a few seconds before saying, "Can we go to your room now? There's too many clothes between us."

"Yes, ma'am," Thatch answers, and the next thing I know he's standing with me in his arms. He's across the apartment and hurrying into his room before I can so much as blink.

"Eager much?" I giggle.

"Yes. Very eager." He sets me down gently on the edge of his bed before pulling off his sweatshirt and the shirt he has on under it. He fumbles with the button of his jeans for a second, but then he's pulling them and his socks off, leaving him in just a pair of black boxers.

I watch, memorizing every inch of him. He flexes, and I know he's doing it because I'm watching.

"You've got too many clothes on." He gives me a quick kiss before gesturing for me to get undressed.

I do as he says, taking off my socks first before standing and unbuttoning and unzipping my jeans, pushing them down my legs and stepping out of them. I glance at Thatch over my shoulder and wink at him. By the heat in his eyes I'd guess he's enjoying the show just as much as I'm enjoying putting it on. I peel off my sweatshirt first and then my shirt, dropping them both to the floor next to my discarded jeans. I reach up to unclasp my bra but he steps closer to me, stilling my hand with his.

"Can I?"

In answer, I turn around so he can reach the clasp on the back. He makes quick work of undoing it, and I peel the straps down my shoulders and drop my bra on top of my other discarded clothes, leaving me in only my underwear. He steps closer to me and wraps his arms around me, pulling me against his chest.

"These are nice," he mumbles, gently squeezing my breasts.

I moan, leaning back against him, his dick nudging against my ass. If I wasn't turned on before, I most certainly am now.

"Are you wet for me?" he whispers in my ear as he trails a hand down my chest and skims his fingers along the edge of my underwear. "Can I take these off?"

I nod against him, and he pushes my underwear down before kneeling in front of me and helping me step out of them. He gazes up at me before slips a finger between my legs to my aching core.

"Fuck. Is all of this for me?"

"Yes."

He removes his finger and I start to protest but he stands up, pulls me close, and continues his exploration between my legs.

He slips a finger inside of me, and my eyes roll into the back of my head at how good it feels. He chuckles and the sound reverberates against me, making goosebumps break out across my skin.

Thatch strokes in and out of me, his thumb finding my clit.

"Thatch," I gasp out. I'm not going to last if he keeps this up. "I'm going to come."

"Mmmm, good," he whispers in my ear before leaning down and kissing along my neck, all the while continuing to stroke in and out of me.

The familiar feeling of an orgasm building starts at the base of my stomach, and a few more pumps and kisses from Thatch has me coming with a yell.

"Beautiful," he says against my neck as he continues to thrust in and out of me.

I'm at a loss for words. All I can do is sag against his chest, grateful that he's holding me up. He finally withdraws his finger, and I can't help the whine that leaves me at the emptiness. He sets me on the edge of bed, and I scoot up until I'm lying against his pillows.

He stares down at me, his eyes raking over my body, and I really hope he likes what he sees. He must because he squeezes his dick through his boxers before shoving them down.

Chapter 14

Thatcher

Having Avery's eyes on me is making me harder and even more turned on. I got to touch her, make her come, give her pleasure, and now I get to fuck her. I grip my cock, stroking it a few times as she watches me.

I still can't believe I have Avery Butler spread out and naked on my bed.

My dream girl.

Is here.

Finally.

After all these years.

If you'd told college aged Thatcher that at thirty-five, he would finally get his dream girl, he wouldn't have believed you.

I grab the new box of condoms—picked up at the grocery store earlier this week—out of my nightstand, open one, and sheath myself.

I give my cock a few strokes for Avery's benefit before taking a deep breath, trying to calm myself down because I want to take this slow.

Make it good for her. Savor her.

Us.

Together for the first time.

"Hi," I whisper as I crawl up the bed and settle over her, balancing on my arms to keep from crushing her, my dick nudging at her hot center.

"Hi, yourself." She brushes her lips against mine, and I lose myself in her kiss. She groans, grinding against me, and I bite my lip at the feel of her wetness along the length of my cock. She pulls away from me breathlessly. "Are you going to put us out of our misery?"

I throw my head back, laughing. "Who said we're miserable?"

"Well, I am." She sticks out her bottom lip in a fake pout.

"Do you want my cock inside of you, Avery?"

"Yes."

That's all the permission I need to line my cock up with her entrance and slowly push inside her.

It's been a while since I've had sex—I've been too busy working and haven't had any desire to date—so I know I won't be able to last long. But I'm going to try because I want to make this good for Avery.

She deserves it.

I don't know how long it's been for her, and from what she's said, it doesn't sound like her ex was the greatest person. She deserves to be taken care of in and out of bed. I want to be the one to do that.

I thrust all the way in and out of her a few times as she grips my shoulders, her legs wrapped around my waist, holding me close.

"You feel so good, sunshine."

"So good, Thatch," she says, her eyes fluttering shut.

"Look at me," I command, and she does as I ask.

I reward her with a smile before capturing one of her nipples between my lips. A groan escapes me as one of her hands falls to my hair, and she scrapes her fingernails against my scalp.

Fucking hell, I'm not going to last long.

"Yes, like that," she says.

I let go of her nipple with a pop and move on to lavish the same attention to the other one. I watch her as she starts to fall apart. The hand not in my hair grips the sheet so hard her knuckles turn white.

"More," she urges me on.

I thrust in and out of her a few more times, feeling her pussy start to flutter around me. The familiar tingle at the base of my spine starts at the sensation. No way am I coming before she does. I reach between us and stroke her clit. That's all she needs to start coming, squeezing my cock with her pussy walls.

"Thatcher," she yells.

A few more thrusts and my orgasm slams into me like a freight train. I collapse on top of her, catching myself with my arms so I don't crush her. We stay like this for a few seconds before I pull out of her.

"You okay?" I finally ask when I catch my breath.

"Perfect." She says before kissing me.

I get lost in the taste of her hips for a few seconds before pulling back. "I'm going to take care of the condom."

I clean myself up quickly in the bathroom before walking back into my bedroom.

"Your turn, sunshine." I lean down and give her a quick kiss.

She yawns and sits up slowly, stretching before sauntering out into the hallway. Once I hear the door shut, I head into the kitchen to get us some water. When I come back into my room, she's sitting on my bed, wearing one of my shirts.

Fucking hell. I can't decide what's sexier—her spread out naked and waiting for me or her wearing one of my shirts.

"Thought you might be thirsty." I hand her her water before taking a sip of my own, watching her over the rim of my glass. She finishes her drink and sets the empty glass on the nightstand.

"Are you going to stand there all night and watch me, or are you going to come over here?"

I smirk at her before getting into bed and lying down on my back, folding my hands under my head, and staring up at her. "Seemed like you enjoy the view."

She blushes and buries her head in her hands.

"Hey. What's wrong?" I ask, sitting up and peeling her hands from her face.

She stares silently down at the blankets. Is she regretting having sex with me? Is she regretting agreeing to be my girlfriend? Did I do something wrong? Did she not enjoy herself?

"Nothing." She blows out a breath. "Sex has never been like that for me."

I puff out my chest. "Because you've never had sex with me." I move so I'm reclining against the headboard.

"I was embarrassed because I wanted to ask when we could do it again, and then I started wondering if I was too eager. And . . ."

I grab her hand and bring it to my hardening cock. "Give me about five minutes." She grips me and starts stroking. "Or sooner if you keep that up."

She takes her shirt off, and I have to bite back a groan at the sight of her naked. How did I get this lucky?

She bats her eyelashes at me, smirking, and I can't help the goofy grin that breaks out on my face. "Sex has never been like that for me either," I admit.

I pull her gently on top of me, and she lets go of my cock as she repositions herself to lay on me. I miss her hand around me instantly, but my eyes flutter shut at feeling her skin against me, her heat on my cock. She rocks against me, and I look up at her.

"Do you want to ride me?"

"I— I've never done that before."

"Well, let's fix that." I reach over to the nightstand where I left the box of condoms and fumble for one.

"Let me."

She leans over me, which puts her tits in my face. Not one to pass up an opportunity to have my girl's nipples in my mouth, I take advantage of her position and suck on one of them. She moans.

"Thatch."

"What?" I ask, letting go of her breast with a silent promise that I'll be back for it and its twin.

"Condom." She holds it up, and I let go of her. She moves off me, tearing open the wrapper as she does. She strokes me a few times before rolling the condom down my dick.

I thrust into her hand. I can't help it. It feels so good to have her touching me. She giggles before climbing on top of me.

I grip her hips, helping her get situated. She lowers herself slowly, and my eyes roll to the back of my head at how good she feels. I know I just had her, but this position feels different.

So much better.

I let go of her and tuck my hands under my head, watching as she lifts off my dick before dropping back down. She starts swirling her hips and I groan. It must feel good to her too based on her moans.

I watch her for a few seconds before reaching up to tweak one of her nipples. Apparently she likes that because her pussy starts squeezing my dick even harder. My other hand finds her clit, and a few swipes has her yelling out her orgasm.

She slumps down onto my chest, and I grip her hips, keeping her steady as she catches her breath.

When she lifts her head and looks at me, I take that as permission to move, flipping us over so she's flat on her back on the bed. I lift her legs and rest them against my chest as I thrust into her. A few seconds later, I'm coming again.

I'm so gone for her.

We may have only been on three dates, but I don't need any more for me to know that I want her.

That I am head over heels for her.

She's my future.

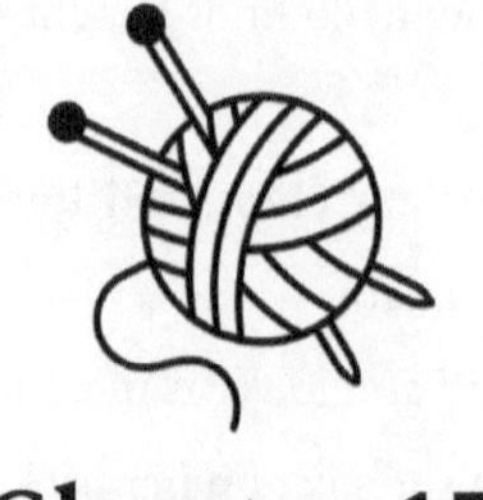

Chapter 15

Avery

I'm not sure what, exactly, wakes me up, but I roll over wide awake. Dim light is visible through the curtains, but it's a Sunday, so there's no reason to get up early. I reach for Thatch, but his side of the bed is empty and cold. I sit up. Maybe he's in the bathroom. Or in the kitchen getting something to drink. We were up kind of late and woke up in the middle of the night to go again.

There's no way he's had enough sleep.

Yawning, I get up, intent on finding him and bringing him back to bed to snuggle and nap for a few hours. I walk out of the bedroom and make a quick stop to use the toilet before continuing down the hallway.

Last night was the best night of my life. And not just because of all the sex Thatcher and I had. Which was a lot.

After our second round, we took a shower, and he made us a late-night snack. Then we got back into bed and fell asleep for a few hours before he woke me up with his head between my legs.

It was the best night of my life because he planned a date he knew I'd love, even if it wasn't his thing. Although I'm pretty sure he was enjoying himself by the end of the game, based on the way he was yelling and cheering.

Everything about Thatcher in the little bit of time we've spent together makes me even more thankful that I took Caro up on her offer to go home with her for Thanksgiving. It takes everything in me not to be angry at myself for not trying harder to reschedule our date in college. For not pursuing him more. All those years wasted. But I can't go there now, or ever. It doesn't do me any good.

"Thatch." I pause in the doorway of his office.

He's sitting at his computer, his back to me, the only light coming from a lamp on the floor. I glance around the room, one wall covered in bookshelves, a dry-erase calendar hung to the left of his desk next to the window. I step closer and see what I assume are clients or projects listed out. Almost every month for the first half of next year has multiple dates and names.

My heart drops.

He's already got so much work planned. I may not know how many hours developing or updating an application or game takes, but I get the feeling that he's way overbooked himself. I knew he was working a lot when we started seeing each other, but I thought it was a temporary thing because he happened to have two projects scheduled at once.

But apparently not.

"Thatcher," I repeat, and this time he lifts his head and turns around to look at me.

I frown. He looks exhausted. Did he sleep at all after he woke me up at two for another round of sex?

"Hey. I didn't wake you, did I?"

"No. What's going on?" I ask, stepping closer to him.

He reaches for me, and I take his hand.

"Trying to catch back up." He gestures behind him with his free hand.

"Are you far behind?"

He sighs, his shoulders dropping. "Not as far as I thought but still a ways to go until this is done."

"You've got a lot of your year already booked." I nod toward the calendar on the wall.

He glances at it before turning back to me. "Yeah, and a couple of smaller projects that might still be trickling in."

"Oh. Do you normally work this much?" I blurt out the question before I can think twice about it.

He stares up at me, visibly swallowing before saying, "Kind of."

"Thatcher…" I take a step back to put space between us.

I need to think for a minute. After everything with my ex, I made a promise to myself that I wouldn't be in a relationship where I came second to my partner's work.

"I love that you're so dedicated to your work, and I know you planned all of these projects"—I gesture to the calendar—"before we started dating, but do you think you'll be able to juggle all of this and us? I'd hate to be the reason you don't get enough sleep. Or neglect other parts of your life."

Or neglect me.

"Sunshine."

"Thatch," I say gently. "The reason I finally asked Chad for a divorce was because he never prioritized me. He would never make plans for too far in the future in case something came up with work. He wouldn't even commit to a weekend away for our fifth wedding anniversary. I understood that his job came first sometimes. Heck, mine did too. But

I was tired of *always* being second. Never being important enough to him."

"That won't happen." He reaches for me, but I move further away from him. I need to be able to think clearly, and he's too distracting when he touches me.

I shake my head. "You don't know that. I'm not asking you to cancel things you've agreed to or change the way you have things planned. I'm saying maybe we should press pause on us until you're not so busy. That we should be friends for now."

"I don't know when that will be." He runs a hand through his hair.

I wrap my arms around myself.

Is this it for us?

Are we over before we even started?

"You can't keep this pace up. Even if I wasn't in the picture. This isn't healthy." I whisper.

He takes off his glasses and rubs his eyes. "There's so much work to be done. Always."

I step forward and place a hand on his shoulder. "I'm sure there is, but what else are you missing out on because you're working so much? What are you trying to prove? Can you hire employees to help you? To take some of the load for you?"

He lets out a bark of laughter before putting his glasses back on and looking up at me. "You sound like Anders. He keeps telling me that."

"Well, maybe you should listen to him." I hook a thumb over my shoulder. "I'm going to go. You look like you're going to be busy for a while."

"No, don't." He stands up and steps toward me. "Please don't leave. How about I make us some breakfast?"

I heave out a breath. I need to do this. Stay firm in my boundaries. "I think it's for the best right now. I care about you. I enjoyed our time together. I want to spend more time with you, but I'm distracting you right now. Did you even sleep?"

"A little. It's fine." He waves a hand around. "I'll sleep later."

I frown at him. "I think I should go. That way you can finish up your work and get some rest."

He sighs, his shoulders drooping. "At least let me drive you."

"No, you stay. I'll get a rideshare. There's no reason for you to drive me all the way home just to turn right around and drive all the way back. That'll be a couple of hours wasted. Stay and work."

"Okay. Can I hug you?" He opens his arms for me, and I step into his embrace, willing myself not to cry.

Why is this relationship already ending when it's barely started?

I hate this.

I could fall in love with him. I know I could. In fact, I might already be a little in love with him. But this is for the best. I pat his back before stepping away, and he lets me go.

I know Thatcher isn't Chad—Chad had other red flags that I missed—but I don't want to wake up in six months, a year, a couple of years, and realize that while we've been together we haven't really *been together* because Thatch has been married to his job and I'm just the third wheel.

"There's coffee in the kitchen. If you want some. While you wait."

"Thanks."

My heart races with every step I take toward his bedroom. I make quick work of getting dressed and requesting a car to take me home. The app says the driver will be here in twenty minutes, so I head to the kitchen and make a cup of coffee under the watchful gaze of Shadow, who watches me from his cat tree in the corner.

Thatcher comes out of his office when I'm finishing my coffee.

"My car is here."

"I'm sorry," he says, coming over to the sink where I'm rinsing my mug.

"I'm sorry too." I grab the towel and dry my hands, then turn to face him.

"Can I kiss you?"

I hesitate for a second before saying, "Yes."

He steps closer to me and kisses me. I wrap my arms around his neck and hold on to him. This feels like a goodbye kiss. I guess it is in a way, but I hope it's temporary.

"I'll walk you out."

I let him lead me to the door, where he hugs me again.

With one last backward glance, I memorize the sight of Thatcher standing in the doorway of his apartment, dressed in a pair of gray joggers and a simple black shirt, glasses perched on his nose, his hair messy from how often he runs his hands through it.

I hope it isn't another fifteen years before I see him again. I hope this isn't the last time I see him.

My eyes burn as I climb into the backseat of the rideshare, and I will myself to not cry. I know I made the right choice telling Thatcher that we needed to pause our relationship until he has more time for me, and for us.

It still doesn't make it any easier.

Chapter 16

Thatcher

I stand in the doorway long after her car has disappeared. Finally, I shake myself out of my stupor, closing and locking the door before heading into the kitchen. Shadow watches me from his perch on the table, where he knows he's not supposed to be. I shake my head at him but am too distraught to tell him to get down.

"What was I supposed to do?" I ask him as I pull out eggs from the fridge.

He says nothing, because of course he doesn't, he's a cat.

I make myself some over-easy eggs and toast, which I eat standing at the counter before going into my office. It's hard to focus on the code in front of me; my mind keeps drifting to Avery and our conversation. She was right to put a pause on our relationship. I hate that she was right, but she was.

There's not a whole lot I can do now. I committed to all of these projects, so I just need to work for as long as it takes to get them completed on time.

Taking a deep breath, I force myself to stop thinking about her and focus on the task I'm working on—testing the code changes I made.

Hours pass and I only get out of my chair when absolutely necessary.

Around two in the morning, I stumble into my bedroom and fall asleep the minute my head hits the pillow.

The next day is much the same—I get up before dawn and work nonstop until I can't keep my eyes open any longer. Luckily, my desk converts to a standing desk, so I'm not sitting for fifteen hours a day. Plus, standing helps me focus. I take a few breaks to do some stretches, push-ups, and jumping jacks when I find myself getting sleepy, but aside from grabbing something quick to eat, getting more water, using the toilet, or checking on Shadow, I don't move.

I repeat the cycle so many times I lose track of what day it is. I'm staring blankly at my screen having just sent off the final package to one of my clients when someone starts pounding on my front door.

"What the fuck?" I grumble, taking my glasses off and rubbing my face.

The banging doesn't stop, so I get up to go see who it is. It'd better be important for the amount of noise they're making at nine at night. A peek through the peephole shows Anders standing on my doorstep, his arms crossed.

"Hey, man," I greet him when I open the door.

"Don't *hey man* me," he says, pushing past me and into my apartment.

"Oh-kay," I mutter, following him into the living room.

"What the hell is going on, Thatcher?" he growls, whirling around to face me.

"What do you mean? I've been working."

"Working? This is way worse than normal, Thatch." He starts pacing. "I've been calling you all day, and you didn't pick up. You stood me up at the gym yesterday. You didn't answer my texts. I thought you were dead."

I chuckle, gesturing toward myself. "Well, I'm not."

"I can see that." He comes to a halt in front of me, frowning at whatever he sees. "When was the last time you took a shower?" he asks, wrinkling his nose. "Or changed your clothes."

I scratch my head.

Yesterday?

The day before?

Maybe...

I don't know.

The days have all run together. I couldn't even tell you what I had for lunch today, if I even ate, let alone when I took a shower last. Which is bad. Really bad, now that I think about it.

"That's what I thought. Go take a shower." He points down the hall. "I'll rummage up something for dinner because if I had to guess, you haven't eaten since this morning. Then we need to talk."

"Is this an intervention?" I grumble.

"Maybe." He glares at me, challenging me to argue.

I shake my head then head to the bathroom and take a shower, which does feel good. Stepping out of it a few minutes later, I catch sight of myself in the mirror and understand what he meant about me looking rough.

I have big black circles under my eyes, which are bloodshot, probably from staring at my computer screen for too many hours, even though my glasses have blue light blocking tint.

I'm pale too. Paler than usual. Rummaging around my medicine cabinet, I find some eye drops. Hopefully they will at least help with the redness.

I take a few deep breaths, suddenly feeling exhausted. Run down. Like I've been knocked over countless times by a bus. All the late nights and early mornings are catching up to me.

My shoulders slump. I can't keep working at this pace. I just can't. As much as the thought of hiring employees scares me, I have to. That or tell my clients I can't take on their projects and need to push some deadlines out, and I don't want to do that. I can't do all the work by myself.

It's not healthy. It's not sustainable. Anders was right. Avery was right. I've been too stubborn to realize it, but it needs to happen.

Strangely, I feel lighter, freer, as I wrap my towel around myself and trek the short distance to my room. I open my dresser drawers to grab clothes and find them pretty empty. Thankfully, I have one last pair of clean underwear and some joggers. I pull them on and grab a shirt from my closet.

Also very empty.

"Fucking hell." I grab my overflowing laundry basket—no wonder I have no clean clothes—and collect the discarded clothes scattered around my room before starting a load of laundry.

I head back and strip my sheets off the bed since I can't remember the last time I washed them. If I'm going to get my shit together, I might as well do it all at once. I drop the dirty sheets and towels on top of the dryer to start once the load in the washer is done.

"Whatcha making?" I ask, walking into the kitchen and taking a seat at the counter.

"Takeout," Anders says, spinning around to face me, two menus in his hand. "Do you feel like Chinese or pizza? Since that's all that's open at this time of night that delivers."

I frown at the menus. "I don't care. Pick."

"Pizza it is."

While he calls in our order, I grab both of us some water since there's nothing to drink in my fridge. I really need to go grocery shopping tomorrow or put in an order for delivery.

"Thirty minutes," Anders says, setting his phone down and taking the glass of water I offer him. "What's going on?" he asks as we make our way into the living room.

"I fucked up," I admit, taking a seat next to him on the couch.

He tilts his head, studying me. "What do you mean?"

I tell him everything that went down between me and Avery.

"She's right. I don't have time for her. Hell, I barely have time for the gym. I need to hire some help." I pinch the bridge of my nose, squeezing my eyes shut and shaking my head. "I should have listened to you. If I had, I wouldn't be in this situation."

Anders heaves out a breath next to me. "Finally. Took you long enough."

I sigh and look over at him. "I should have done this months ago. I feel like shit. I don't want to lose her. If I haven't already."

My stomach drops at the thought of Avery moving on with someone else. I want her to be happy, but I was really hoping that it would be with me.

"I don't think you've lost her. At least not yet. I'm glad you finally came to your senses." He gives me a small smile. "I'll get you the names and numbers of a few recruiters I know." He pauses, watching me. "I'm sure they'll be able to find you a couple of good developers. It might take a little while with Christmas almost here. But you have got to take better care of yourself in the meantime."

"I know." I sink back against the couch, feeling the weight of all of the stress and lack of sleep over the past week. What the hell have I done to myself?

"And answer your damn phone next time so I don't think something bad has happened to you."

I blow out a breath, running a hand through my hair. "The battery is probably dead."

He shakes his head at me. "Where is it? If I'm worried about you, what do you think your family is thinking? Or Avery? Maybe she's trying to get a hold of you and can't." He gets to his feet, presumably to go get my phone.

"Top drawer of my desk," I call after him.

What did I do to deserve such a good friend?

"Plugged it in. You okay?" he asks as he returns to his seat next to me.

"I will be. Thank you for being concerned about me. For coming over."

"Always. I know you'd do the same for me."

I smile at him, unsure of what to say. I'm saved from having to figure it out by the knock at the door. I get to my feet, suddenly starving, and follow Anders into the kitchen. He pays the delivery guy, and we dig into our meal.

I feel like the weight has been lifted off my chest knowing that I made the right decision about my business. Now, I can only hope that I didn't make that decision too late. That I still have a chance with Avery, because the time we've spent together, even just laughing and talking at my parent's house, was some of the most fun I've had in years.

This time, I don't plan to let my dream girl get away.

Chapter 17

Avery

"You promise he's okay?" I ask Caro as we're sitting down to eat dinner.

"He will be. He looked like shit, but it sounds like he hit rock bottom and realized he needed to make a change. I'm not sure what Anders said to him. As much as the man drives me insane, I love him for the way he stands by Thatcher and doesn't let him get away with shit. Especially when that shit is not taking care of himself."

I wanted to go with Caro today when she drove over to her brother's apartment—he finally called her after ignoring her calls all week—but she told me she needed to handle it by herself. That if I came with her, he might get confused about the boundary I'd set in regard to us.

It's a relief to hear that Thatcher finally realized he can't do it all and doesn't want to keep trying to. That he's going to hire some help. Hopefully. I think. So he says.

"Do you think he really will?"

"Will what?" Caro asks before shoveling a spoonful of chili into her mouth.

"Hire employees. Off-load some of his work."

She lifts one shoulder in half a shrug. "I think so, but we'll see. He's already talked to a couple of recruiters and was working on a job description when I got there. I've also never seen him that..." She waves her hand around. "Worn down."

"I feel bad I walked away from him," I say, staring down at my empty bowl.

"No." She puts her hand on top of mine, and I meet her eyes. "If you hadn't, I don't think he would have changed his mind about hiring help. He would have continued to try to juggle your relationship and work and eventually burnt out even worse. You had every right to set those boundaries. You weren't asking anything unreasonable of him. What girlfriend would be fine with her boyfriend working basically all the time? It wouldn't have been healthy for either of you."

I blow out a breath. "I know. I still feel bad."

"Don't." Caro stands, collecting both of our empty dishes, and turns to walk into the kitchen. "He's my brother, and I love him, and I want him to be happy. But I want you to be happy too. If it makes you feel any better, I'm proud of you for setting boundaries with him and telling him what you expect out of a relationship."

I give her a tight-lipped grin before finishing my wine and helping her clean up. As I'm getting settled on the couch with my knitting project, my phone dings with a text message. Assuming it's my mom wanting to talk about Christmas, I grab it from the coffee table and unlock it. My mouth drops open as I read the text from Thatcher.

Thatch:

> Hey, sunshine. I'm sure by now you've talked to Caro. If not, the short story is that I realized you were right. Everyone was. I can't keep doing things the way I have been. I need to hire some help. Anders put me in touch with some recruiters he knows, and I'm hoping they can find me someone quickly. I miss you. Talk soon.

I read his text a couple of times, trying to figure out how to respond. I want to call him and hear his voice. Get in my car and drive over to his apartment. But I don't.

Me:

> Caro told me. I'm so proud of you. If there's anything I can do to help, please let me know. I miss you too.

I set my phone on the coffee table and concentrate on my knitting. Caro comes into the living room a few minutes later and turns on a reality show.

It's hard to focus on anything because I can't stop thinking about Thatcher and what he said in his text. What Caro told me. Because I know I'm one day closer to seeing him again.

Chapter 18

Thatcher

I hesitate, my hand hovering next to the door of Avery's apartment. I know she's home—Caro told me she would be—and I also know my twin is gone for the night, at her friend Mary's house. Even though she won't admit it, I'm pretty sure Caro specifically planned her New Year's Eve so she wouldn't be home.

It's been a few weeks since Avery walked out of my apartment, and aside from the one text message I sent her I haven't talked to her. Caro told me that she's doing okay, and I'm grateful for my sister's updates.

I raise my hand and, this time, knock on the door before stepping back and hoping that she isn't already in bed.

"Thatcher," Avery says, her voice hitching as she opens the door. "Caro's not home." The words come out in a whisper as she stares at me.

I swallow suddenly unsure of what to say or how to say it. I take a deep breath praying that she doesn't turn me away. Tell me to leave.

I finally find my voice and say, "I know. I'm here for you. I hope that's okay." I hold up a bottle of champagne. "Happy New Year's Eve," I add, like she doesn't know what day it is.

"Come in." She holds the door open for me.

I hand her the champagne, and she takes it while I slip off my boots and hang my jacket on the hook by the front door.

"I hired two contractors. They start next week," I blurt out.

She stares at me, blinking a few times, and I wonder if this was a bad idea. But before I can run out of the apartment like I really want to, she flings her arms around me. I laugh, hugging her. I missed her. A lot.

Letting go of me, she steps back, her eyes raking down my body, and I hope she likes what she sees. I've been taking better care of myself—eating proper meals, going to the gym with Anders, and even spending a little bit of time outside every day. I'm still not getting enough sleep, but I'm working on it.

"I wish I'd known you were coming over. I would have made an effort."

"It's fine. I wanted to surprise you." I take in her outfit—a pair of black leggings, a long-sleeve shirt that leaves no room for me to guess whether or not she's wearing a bra—she's not—and a pair of fuzzy socks.

"Come on, let's go sit." She points toward the living room. "Should I open this? Sounds like we have something to celebrate." She holds up the bottle of champagne.

I nod, letting her lead me into the kitchen, loving the feel of her hand in mine. All I want to do is haul her into my arms, kiss her senseless, and suggest we leave the champagne for later and instead reacquaint ourselves with each other's bodies. But I don't do that. I need to know where we stand first.

"I'm hoping you'll give me a second chance," I tell her when we're in the kitchen and she's grabbing wine glasses from the cabinet. "I'll still probably be really busy until I get my new employees up to speed. I'll probably still work a lot during the week. But I promise, no more late nights or weekends." She goes to say something, but I hold up a hand, and she gestures for me to continue as she opens the bottle of champagne with a pop. "Unless there's some sort of emergency that can't wait. I want to do better. For you. For me too."

She stares at me for a beat before setting the bottle down and launching herself at me. I catch her and kiss the shit out of her. When we pull away from each other a few minutes later, her eyes are shining with tears, and I think mine are too.

"Yes, please, boyfriend. I missed you."

"I missed you too, girlfriend. Thank you for being patient with me." I blow out a breath.

I hate that we had to go through that. I hate that I couldn't spend Christmas with her. That we missed out on more time when we could have been together, but at the end of the day, she did what she needed to do, and it was a wake-up call for me.

"I'm glad you figured your shit out." She kisses me again. "I think I'm in love with you, Thatcher Wells."

"You think you're in love with me?" I chuckle. "Well, that's fine because I know I'm in love with you, Avery Butler." I pull her into my arms and hold her close.

"I love you, Thatch," she whispers.

"I love you too, sunshine." I kiss her again. I'll never get tired of feeling her lips pressed against mine, tasting her. "Want to put the champagne in the fridge and take this party into your bedroom?"

"But it'll go flat," she says, pretending to pout.

I roll my eyes. "Fine, we can take it with us, but I'm not sure how much we'll be drinking." I shift so she can feel how hard I am for her. "I missed you, and I'd like to make up for wasted time."

"Yes. Let's do that instead. Champagne. Fridge."

I grab the bottle and put it in the fridge before letting her lead me to her bedroom so we can make up for lost time and I can show her exactly how much I love her and her body.

A couple of hours later, once I've shown her twice how much I've missed her and we're snuggled under the covers in her bedroom, I say something that's been on my mind for a while. "I'm so glad Caro invited you to go with her for Thanksgiving. I thought I was seeing things. I hadn't slept well the night before, and I wondered if I was hallucinating or dreaming."

"And to think I almost didn't go."

"I'd like to think that eventually we'd have met. That things would have worked out in the end."

"I hope so. How about that champagne now? Since it's almost midnight." Avery climbs out of bed, grabs my shirt from the floor, and pulls it on as she walks out of her room.

This is the best New Year's Eve ever. I don't think anything will ever top tonight. Well, maybe our wedding day. Because, yes, I'm already planning that.

She returns with the champagne and two glasses before I can get out of bed. She pours us each a glass and settles next to me.

"Do you ever want to get married again?" I blurt out.

She turns, staring at me. "Are you proposing to me, Thatcher?"

I smirk. "No. Do you want me to?"

She takes a sip of her champagne. "When Chad and I got divorced, I was convinced I didn't ever want to get married again. But now, yeah, I think I'd like to. Only to you, though."

"Noted." I can't help the massive smile that breaks out on my face.

"But let's enjoy dating for a while first?"

"Okay," I answer, taking a sip of my champagne, although I'm already planning how and when I'm going to propose to her.

Because this woman will be my wife.

One day.

Epilogue

I look around the living room where Mom, Dad, Hudson, Avery's parents, and Anders are seated. Everything is going according to plan. Caro asked Avery to help her look for something in her room, and that's when I snuck Avery's parents into the house. She doesn't know that they're here for Thanksgiving. She thinks they went on another cruise like last year.

"Here they come." I wave my hands around as footsteps ring out from the stairwell.

I pat my pocket where the ring sits. It's been a pain in the ass to hide it from Avery for the past few months, especially since we live together. But it's all worth it. I can't wait to see the look on her face in a few minutes. As long as she doesn't say no. Not that I think she will.

"What's everyone . . ." she says, glancing around the room. "Mom. Dad. What are you guys doing here? I thought you were on a Mediterranean cruise."

"Surprise," Amy, Avery's mom, says, standing and hugging her daughter.

Once Avery has said hello to her parents, she comes over to me in the middle of the living room.

"What's going on, Thatch?"

"Avery," I say, getting down on one knee and pulling the diamond ring, which I picked out with Caro's help a few months ago, from my pocket. Taking her hand, I meet her eyes. "Avery Butler, my dream girl, I think I've been falling for you since that first day in English Lit when you sat down next to me. Then when I finally got up the courage to ask you out, Mother Nature said no way. I kicked myself for years for not trying harder when our date got canceled. When I ran into you last Thanksgiving in this very house, I thought I was dreaming. Or dead." Everyone laughs. "But thankfully I wasn't. This past year has been the best of my life. And it's all thanks to you. I love you, sunshine. Will you marry me?"

"Yes! Yes, Thatcher," Avery says, tearing up. I slip the ring onto her finger and stand and kiss my fiancée. Everyone cheers and claps around us, but that all fades into the background as I kiss my dream girl.

"I love you," she whispers. "This past year has been the best of my life too."

"Good. I'm glad. It's only going to get better, sunshine."

"Who wants some champagne?" Anders asks, and we turn our attention to him.

I'm glad he's here today too. I wouldn't be here with my fiancée if it wasn't for him, and for that, I'll be ever grateful.

He walks over and hands me a glass of champagne, clapping me on the shoulder. "Congrats."

"Thanks."

"Anytime." He turns to give my fiancée a hug.

"Welcome to the family," Alex, Avery's dad, says when it's his turn to congratulate me. "Take care of her." He nods toward Avery, standing with her mom, my mom, and Caro.

"I will," I promise.

There's nothing I won't do for that woman. I plan to show her over and over for the rest of our lives how important she is to me and how she's my number one. Because she is.

Over the summer, I hired two permanent full-time developers to take over a lot of the day-to-day development work I did, and it's been the best decision ever. I still get to code when I want to, but for the most part, my role has transitioned to client interfacing and project management. It also means that I'm working a more regular schedule, although occasionally I have to put in a long day when there's an issue, but that's becoming less and less often.

I've even been talking to Anders about the possibility of bringing on a part-time project manager to handle some of the day-to-day management. Something I didn't think I would ever be okay with, but the more time I spend with Avery, the more I dream of us being able to take off for weeks or even a month at a time so we can travel.

One thing at a time though.

Right now, we've got an engagement to celebrate and a wedding to plan. I look over at Avery, who is chatting with my sister and mom.

My dream girl is finally mine.

Life couldn't get any better.

Thank you so much for reading Thatcher and Avery's story. If you enjoyed it, please consider leaving a rating/review on Amazon and/or Goodreads or Storygraph.

Want more of Thatcher and Avery? Click here or scan the QR code below for a link to the Bonus Epilogue.

Ready for another holiday novella? Turn the page to read the first chapter of Wishing For You: A New Year's Eve novella available here.

Have you met Hunter and Madison? Their novel – Hot Shot (book 1 in the Orlando Storm series) is available now.

Chapter One - Wishing For You

Caroline

I can't believe I let Mary talk me into going on a blind date the week before Christmas. Who even goes out on a first date this time of year? No one. This is when you're supposed to be getting together with friends and family, not having dinner with someone you don't know.

I glance around the restaurant, noticing that most of the tables are full even though it's a Monday night. I'm not surprised because Blue Diamond is popular. I've tried to get reservations multiple times, but the earliest I could ever get was next fall. Maybe it's silly, but part of the reason I even agreed to this is because we're having dinner here. I'm breaking a cardinal rule of mine too because usually I insist on meeting for drinks for a first date. That way, if it sucks, I only have to suffer for an hour or so. But I couldn't pass up coming here. The food alone is worth it.

Does that make me desperate?

Maybe I am.

I've only been out with a handful of guys since I deleted all the dating apps from my phone last Thanksgiving. The apps hadn't led to any relationships, so I decided to take a break from them which led to my lack of dates over the past year. Maybe that's another reason why I agreed to this.

Sighing, I adjust the sleeve of my dress and fidget with the copy of *Pride and Prejudice* that's next to me on the table.

The book was Mary's idea. She said that's how Will, my date, would identify me. I guess telling him to look for a woman in her late thirties sitting alone at a table for two with a glass of red wine in front of her wasn't good enough.

Although, I'm not sure how he'll miss me since everyone else at the restaurant is with someone.

I take a sip of my wine. Resisting the urge to pull my phone out and scroll social media to distract myself, I take a few deep breaths to slow my racing heart. I'm nervous because I don't know what to expect.

When I went out with guys I'd met online, I had gotten to know them a little bit because we'd chatted through whatever app we'd met on. Now, all I have to go off is what Mary told me—that her cousin, Will, is my age, single, handsome, polite, and has a job. I have no idea what his likes or dislikes are. If we even have anything in common.

"Caroline." A voice breaks into my thoughts.

A voice I'd recognize anywhere.

I turn, glaring at the guy—Anders, my twin brother's best friend and my self-proclaimed enemy, who is standing at my table dressed in one of his perfectly tailored and likely expensive black suits with a bouquet of Gerbera daisies in his hand.

Great. He gets a front row seat to my awkward first date.

As that thought enters my head, I register why he's holding flowers and do a double take.

"No. No fucking way." I cross my arms.

"Hi Caroline." Anders pulls out the chair across from me, unbuttons his suit jacket, revealing the matching vest underneath, and takes a seat, setting the flowers on top of the book.

"You've got to be kidding me." I squeeze my eyes shut, praying when I open them that this is a dream.

But it's not.

This is real fucking life.

"Mary said my date's name was Will. No way I'd have agreed to this if I'd known it was *you*."

Fuck.

Me.

Why, universe?

Why?

What have I done to warrant this cruel bad joke? If you can even call it a bad joke. Nightmare, maybe?

Before Anders can respond the waiter comes over. "Welcome, sir. What can I get for you to drink?"

"Oh, he's not staying." I wave a hand at Anders, who has the audacity to smirk.

"A whiskey on the rocks please," he says.

The waiter glances from me to Anders, clearly confused.

"Fine." I huff. Giving in mostly because I don't want to cause a scene in the middle of a crowded restaurant. "One drink." I hold up a finger and give Anders a pointed look. He'd better get the hint.

The waiter disappears, leaving us alone.

Anders adjusts his watch, his wrists peeking out from beneath his white button-down and black suit jacket, and there's something sexy about that.

Nope.

No.

Anders is not sexy.

He meets my gaze and has the nerve to wink at me.

"My first name is William. I'm Anders because Anderson is my middle name," he says, finally answering my question.

Before I can say anything in response, our waiter reappears and sets Anders's drink down in front of him. "I'll give you a few minutes to decide if you're staying past drinks." He all but sprints away from the table.

"Oh, I'm staying," Anders mutters, picking up his menu and perusing it.

"No, you're not." I grab my glass of wine and take a sip.

He peers at me, frowning. "Why do you hate me?"

I ignore his question, instead asking my own. "Weren't you curious when Mary told you the woman she was setting you up with was named Caroline?"

He shrugs, turning his attention back to the menu in his hand. I glare at him, refusing to even consider choosing what I might like to eat because, oh no, this dinner is not happening. He's finishing his drink and leaving. As if sensing that I'm watching him, he puts the menu down.

"Caroline is a pretty common name. I didn't think much of it. But we're here now. We might as well enjoy dinner. Especially when it's so hard to get a reservation. I hear the seafood is excellent if you're not sure what to get."

"You're so fucking uptight and stuck up," I blurt out.

"Excuse me?" Anders raises his eyebrows, studying me, before taking a sip of his drink.

"You asked why I dislike you. That's why."

Well, that and other reasons, but he doesn't need to know that. He doesn't need to hear how I liked him immediately when my brother introduced him to me at a Fourth of July party.

That I was on my way over to talk to him when I overheard him talking to another guy about me. I didn't hear the whole conversation, but I heard enough to know that my initial judgment of him was inaccurate.

"I'm not uptight. Or stuck up, *Caroline*. I also don't buy that answer, but I'll let it slide. For now."

I shake my head, choosing to ignore the second part of his statement. "You wanted to have dinner here."

I gesture around the fancy restaurant, everyone dressed to the nines, including me, the lights dimmed low, soft ambient music playing over the speakers, every table set with *cloth* napkins, not a plastic utensil, paper napkin, or any plastic dishware in sight. The cheapest item on the menu, that's not a side salad or cup of soup, is fifty dollars.

He frowns, glancing around. "I heard the food was fantastic, which is why I picked it. Do you not want to eat here? We can go somewhere else." He starts to push his chair away from the table as if to leave.

I blow out a breath. "I've heard that too," I admit. "I've wanted to try this place for ages." Ugh, I am not giving in. Nope. I refuse to let my anger toward him dissolve based on him offering to go somewhere else for dinner.

"The perks of knowing the owner." He leans back in his seat, picking his menu up again. "Let's order, and then we can talk."

My stomach rumbles, and I lose the energy to fight with him about eating together. I sigh and finally pick up my menu.

"Might as well get use out of that sexy dress anyways," he mutters, and my heart skips a beat.

I ignore it, instead focusing on deciding what to eat for dinner. I settle on blackened, freshly caught cod with rice pilaf and vegetables.

"So," Anders says, steepling his hands on the table and leveling me a look once the waiter has taken our orders and disappears. "Let's get back to the topic at hand."

"Oh." I raise an eyebrow, something I've perfected over the years and that drives my twin, Thatcher, insane because he can't do it. "What topic is that? The fact that I never knew your real name was William and therefore got tricked into a blind date with you? Or the fact that we're here together at all?"

Anders picks up his whiskey glass, swirling it around a few times, and I can't help staring at his hands, at his fingers and how big they are. And how they might feel . . . nope, not going there. I clench my thighs together, trying to ignore the ache.

I haven't had sex in a while, and he's arguably very attractive. You'd have to be blind not to see that. That's all. Besides, it's Anders for fuck's sake. I don't like the guy. I blush as I shake myself out of my stupor. He smirks, and I roll my eyes before distracting myself with a sip of my wine.

"My father's name is William, so I've never gone by it."

"Oh?" I perk up. This is the first I've heard about his father, his family in general. Not that I care. Nope, I don't. I'm still here because the wine is good, and the food is hopefully going to be even better.

"Yeah. William Anderson Cunningham III. That's me."

Cunningham, that name sounds familiar, but I can't put my finger on where I know it from. Maybe from hearing Thatcher say it. "Well, if you go by Anders, why does Mary call you Will?"

He huffs out a laugh. "To fuck with me. Growing up she used to call me William Anderson or The Third to get under my skin. It took a good many years to convince her to call me Will. Heaven forbid I ask her to call me Anders."

The waiter chooses that moment to bring our dinner, and after making sure we have everything, he leaves us to enjoy our food. I stifle the moan that wants to leave my mouth the minute I take a bite of my cod. Whoever told Anders the seafood was fantastic wasn't kidding.

"Do you really not like me?" Anders asks after a few moments of silence. "Or are you saying that to get under my skin?"

I take a deep breath, setting my fork down and staring at my plate for a few seconds before speaking. "You rub me the wrong way. I don't know what my brother sees in you. You're so uptight and stiff."

"I can assure you I'm not uptight, and the only thing that's stiff is the thing that should be."

Did he make a joke?

I peek up at him and am met with the look of a man who is trying to stifle a laugh, his blue eyes sparkling. I open my mouth to snark back, but we're interrupted.

"Hello, son."

Wishing For You is available now, here.

Also by Marissa James

Orlando Storm Series

Hot Shot – Hunter & Madison

Break Out – Brody & Aubrey

Golden Goal – Holt & Rebecca

Blue Line – Wes & Hadley

For You Series

Falling For You: A Thanksgiving Novella – Avery & Thatcher

Wishing For You: A New Year's Eve Novella – Caroline & Anders

Acknowledgements

To my husband: I love you. Thank you for supporting me on this journey and for encouraging me when I was ready to give up. I could not have done this without you.

Ashley: Thank you for your help and encouragement this past year and while writing this book. I couldn't have done it without you. Thank you for your friendship.

Jordan: Thank you for creating an amazing cover. You took some vague ideas and created a gorgeous cover that I absolutely love.

To my Beta readers: Thank you being part of my team. I am so appreciate your suggestions and feedback. This book wouldn't be what it is without each and every one of you.

Laura, my editor and Trinity, my proofreader: Thank you for giving this book a fresh set of eyes. I appreciate each of you helping me make this book the best it can be.

To my ARC readers and every reader: Thank you for taking a chance on me once again. For being excited for this book, for telling your friends about it. For your messages, reviews, comments, and posts on social media. I still can't believe there are people reading my books and loving them.

About the Author

Marissa James grew up reading books and dreaming of being an author. She finally decided to pursue her dream of being a published author in 2022. She loves to write happily ever afters with a perfect blend of emotion and steamy romance. When she's not writing, she can be found working her day job, reading romance novels, watching hockey, or hanging out with her husband.

Website: www.marissajamesauthor.com

www.ingramcontent.com/pod-product-compliance
Lightning Source LLC
Chambersburg PA
CBHW051457130726
47987CB00005B/2349